"So what you're saying is, you don't find me attractive,"

Tom said.

"Don't be silly. You're a total hunk. I just don't want a girl/guy relationship right now." And the twinges he caused were merely meaningless artifacts of her first girlhood crush. Irrelevant holdovers. Nothing to worry about.

"Girl/guy?" The corners of his mouth edged up in a reluctant smile.

"You know what I mean. I need to get my act together.... I'm gonna be somebody's mother in a month. I have important things to do. I can't be distracted by a bunch of mushy stuff...." She flapped her hand imperiously until he finally pulled her up. How could she stand on her own two feet when she couldn't even get off her backside without help?

Dear Reader,

We've been trying to capture what Silhouette Romance means to our readers, our authors and ourselves. In canvassing some authors, I've heard wonderful words about the characteristics of a Silhouette Romance novel—innate tenderness, lively, thoughtful, fun, emotional, hopeful, satisfying, warm, sparkling, genuine and affirming.

It pleases me immensely that our writers are proud of their line and their readers! And I hope you're equally delighted with their offerings. Be sure to drop a line or visit our Web site and let us know what we're doing right—and any particular favorite topics you want to revisit.

This month we have another fantastic lineup filled with variety and strong writing. We have a new continuity—HAVING THE BOSS'S BABY! Judy Christenberry's *When the Lights Went Out...* starts off the series about a powerful executive's discovery that one woman in his office is pregnant with his child. But who could it be? Next month Elizabeth Harbison continues the series with *A Pregnant Proposal*.

Other stories for this month include Stella Bagwell's conclusion to our MAITLAND MATERNITY spin-off. Go find *The Missing Maitland*. Raye Morgan's popular office novels continue with *Working Overtime*. And popular Intimate Moments author Beverly Bird delights us with an amusing tale about *Ten Ways To Win Her Man*.

Two more emotional titles round out the month. With her writing partner, Debrah Morris wrote nearly fifteen titles for Silhouette Books as Pepper Adams. Now she's on her own with *A Girl, a Guy and a Lullaby*. And Martha Shields's dramatic stories always move me. Her *Born To Be a Dad* opens with an unusual, powerful twist and continues to a highly satisfying ending!

Enjoy these stories, and keep in touch.

Mary-Theresa Hussey

Mary-Theresa Hussey,
Senior Editor

Please address questions and book requests to:
Silhouette Reader Service
U.S.: 3010 Walden Ave., P.O. Box 1325, Buffalo, NY 14269
Canadian: P.O. Box 609, Fort Erie, Ont. L2A 5X3

A Girl, a Guy and a Lullaby

DEBRAH MORRIS

SILHOUETTE *Romance*®

Published by Silhouette Books

America's Publisher of Contemporary Romance

Dedication:

This book is dedicated to my husband, Keith. Thank you, honey, for believing in me, and for having the grace not to look too nervous when I announced I was quitting my job to write.

Acknowledgment:

Special thanks to Carla Ulbrich, a talented and award-winning singer, songwriter and guitarist. She graciously answered my music questions and inspired me with her songs.

 SILHOUETTE BOOKS

ISBN 0-373-19549-4

A GIRL, A GUY AND A LULLABY

Copyright © 2001 by Debrah Morris

This edition published by arrangement with Harlequin Books S.A.

® and TM are trademarks of Harlequin Books S.A., used under license. Trademarks indicated with ® are registered in the United States Patent and Trademark Office, the Canadian Trade Marks Office and in other countries.

Visit Silhouette at www.eHarlequin.com

Printed in U.S.A.

DEBRAH MORRIS

Before embarking on a solo writing career, Debrah Morris coauthored over twenty romance novels as one half of the Pepper Adams/Joanna Jordan writing team. She's been married for twenty-three years, and between them, she and her husband have five children. She's changed careers several times in her life, but finds she much prefers writing to working. She loves to hear from readers, who can contact her at P.O. Box 522, Norman, OK 73070-0522.

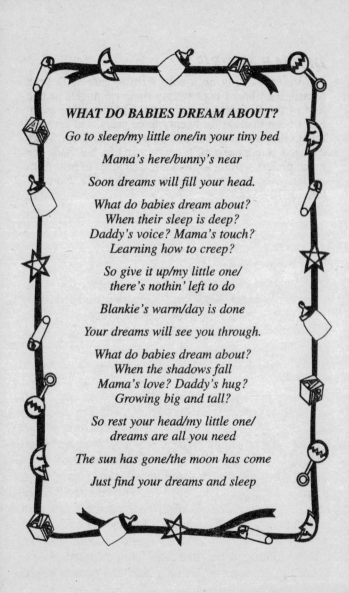

WHAT DO BABIES DREAM ABOUT?

Go to sleep/my little one/in your tiny bed

Mama's here/bunny's near

Soon dreams will fill your head.

What do babies dream about?
When their sleep is deep?
Daddy's voice? Mama's touch?
Learning how to creep?

So give it up/my little one/
there's nothin' left to do

Blankie's warm/day is done

Your dreams will see you through.

What do babies dream about?
When the shadows fall
Mama's love? Daddy's hug?
Growing big and tall?

So rest your head/my little one/
dreams are all you need

The sun has gone/the moon has come

Just find your dreams and sleep

Chapter One

Like bungee jumping off bridges or hiking the Himalayas, cross-country bus trips were best undertaken by those with a taste for adventure. Such endeavors were not meant for the lily-livered or the terminally pregnant. Since she currently qualified in both categories, Ryanne Rieger had to wonder. What the heck had she been thinking?

It was late. She was tired. And no matter how much she wriggled in her seat, she couldn't shift her enormous belly into a less tormenting position. Frustrated, she kicked off her shoes. When had they morphed from high-fashion sandals into medieval torture devices?

And when had they crossed the equator? Humid night air streamed through the open window with the refreshment factor of a wool blanket. Fanning one's self with an empty bag of chips was no substitute for conked-out air-conditioning.

Rifling through her tote bag for a ponytail elastic, Ryanne finger-combed her long hair and twisted it into a dark, off-kilter wad. Then she tried stretching from side to side, but nothing would ease the nagging pain in her lower back.

At least her restless squirming hadn't disturbed the elderly Native American beside her. Since falling asleep in Arkansas, the old fellow had not moved, snored, burped or breathed. Apparently he suffered from a rare medical condition in which extreme heat and bone-rattling movement induced clinical relaxation.

"Ouch." Ryanne winced as her unborn child commenced clogdancing on her bladder. The kid was good. Made the Lord of the Dance look like a lead-footed serf. "Please, baby," she whispered. "I can't handle any more major discomfort."

She glanced at the rear of the bus and considered her options. No way was she going into that undersize closet they called a rest room. Even if she managed to squeeze in, she couldn't maneuver. She'd get stuck, and they'd have to use the jaws of life to pry her out. As entertaining as that might be for her fellow travelers, she'd had enough indignity in her life lately, thank you very much.

She would just tough it out. Soldier on. She could do it, if the baby canceled the encore and she banished all thoughts of liquids. She'd just about perfected a mental movie of sand dunes and desert vistas, when a hungry soul across the aisle popped the lid off a snack can of Vienna sausages.

Like an evil genie released from a lamp, the swirling aroma commingled with the scent of whatever the motion-sick two-year-old had yakked up behind her. After merging with the powerful cologne of the stout gentleman in front, it made a beeline for Ryanne's sensitive nostrils.

Ah, eau de mass transit. Capable of altering genetic structure and undermining the democratic process.

Her stomach lurched and she fought back the familiar wave. She slumped in the seat, feeling uncharacteristically sorry for herself. She was alone, pregnant, penniless. And on her way back to Brushy Creek in disgrace.

Nausea was an unnecessary redundancy.

She'd left home the day after high school graduation, confident she would set Nashville on fire. She'd had big plans. She would play her fiddle at the Grand Ole Opry. Fend off big-name stars clamoring to perform her songs. Become the darling of country music. She was supposed to have a freaking Grammy by now.

Confident? Try delusional.

Five years and hard experience had taught her that life possessed a number of painful ways to humble dreamers and impose reality. She didn't have many dreams left, but she'd gladly relinquish the last of her illusions just to get off this bus.

And soon.

"Hey, driver. How much farther to Brushy Creek?" She couldn't take many more bumps like that last one, and she was seriously thinking of iced tea.

"Comin' up now, little lady." The driver shifted gears, and the brakes squealed as he pulled off the road.

She stared out into unrelieved darkness. Brushy Creek, Oklahoma, population 983, had been a wide place in the road when she left. Had it graduated to full-fledged ghost town in her absence? Where were the lights? The people?

More to the point, where was the nearest rest room?

The door opened with a swoosh and the driver hopped out. Ryanne set the carryall on the floor and pulled her fiddle case down from the overhead compartment.

Where the heck were her shoes? Unable to bend over, she poked her feet under the surrounding seats, blindly searching for the strappy little numbers that had so much in common with her ex-husband.

Like him, they'd been taken home on impulse, had never really fit, and ended up causing more pain than their cute looks justified.

"Lady, this ain't a regular stop. If you're gettin' off, you best be gettin'. I gotta schedule to keep." The driver, obviously a man with a mission, had unloaded her suitcases from the baggage area and climbed back in his seat.

"Tonight sometime," he muttered.

"Fine!" Forget the stupid shoes, they weren't *that* cute. Ryanne grabbed her fiddle case and tote and padded barefoot and apologetic down the long aisle, bumping into everyone she passed. At the door she looked back. The old man still hadn't moved.

She stood in the doorwell and spoke to the driver. "I know you have a schedule and all, but you might want to check that passenger back there for a pulse."

Stepping out in the dark onto the still-warm pavement, she landed squarely in a giant glob of discarded chewing gum. Teetering on one foot, she scraped the sticky mess on the curb. Surely there was a special table in hell reserved for the careless masticators of the world.

She was spun around by a violent jerk, accompanied by the sound of ripping fabric. Dismayed, she watched the bus angle back onto the road with a thin strip of her voluminous maternity dress waving from the door.

What next? She stared up and challenged the night sky. Cue the unexpected cloudburst. Dispense the lightning bolts. And while you're at it, how about some golfball size hail? Come on. Show me what's behind door number three.

Then she recalled the words of Birdie Hedgepath. Her Cherokee foster mother had often told her, *If you don't stand up and laugh at the curves life throws you, you'll fall down and cry.*

But don't laugh too hard, she amended, until you find that toilet.

She looked around. Darkness everywhere. And no sign of life. There were no public facilities, so she'd have to settle for some nice bushy bushes and pray she wouldn't step in anything else.

"It's funny," a deep voice drawled behind her. "But up until now, I thought 'barefoot and pregnant' was just a figure of speech."

Ryanne peered into the void as a man emerged from the shadows, all wide shoulders and long legs. His clothes were the color of the night. Dark shirt. Dark jeans. Dark hat.

Oh, goody. A cowboy vampire comedian. Just what she needed to make the evening complete.

She couldn't see his face, but she heard the smirky grin in his voice. The smirk was the last straw. She could not have stopped the words, even if she'd wanted to. They spewed forth, hot enough to peel paint.

"You think it's funny? I guarantee there is nothing even remotely amusing about any of this. I just spent two days on a bus ride from hell. With puking children, sweaty people, and no air-conditioning.

"I'm tired. I'm hot. Every muscle and bone in my body aches. And as you so cleverly observed, I'm pregnant. You know something? When I got on that bus, I had shoes. I lost 'em. But, hey! It doesn't matter. They don't fit. Because, like the rest of me, my feet are beyond humongous, and I am retaining enough water to irrigate every cornfield in Oklahoma. Do you see how *not* funny that is, cowboy?"

"Yes, ma'am."

The clod didn't even have the manners to conceal what was obviously a bald-faced lie. That only fueled the fire. "But the fun doesn't stop there. I just stepped in a wad of bubble gum the size of a cow patty!" Her final shriek fell well within the vocal range of howler monkeys.

"Let me see."

The man's quiet request had a cold-water-in-the-face effect on Ryanne. She stared at him. Or at least in his direction. She really couldn't see him very well. "What?"

"Give me your foot."

Under normal circumstances she would not consider surrendering her foot, or any other body part, to a total stranger. However, these were not normal circumstances. Like much of the bus trip, they bordered on the surreal.

The total stranger in question pulled a red bandanna from his pocket and moistened it liberally with his tongue. Straddling her uplifted foot like a blacksmith shoeing a mare, he rubbed her sticky sole until it tingled.

She clung to his rock-hard arm for balance. His rear end was backed up against her, and the wave of heat she felt had nothing to do with ambient temperature.

"That's better." He finished scrubbing and returned her foot to the sidewalk.

"Did you just spit on me?" She still felt off-balance. Even with both feet firmly on the ground. When she noticed where her hand lingered, she snatched it away.

"I reckon so." His words constituted a verbal shrug.

"Well, thanks. I think."

"Happy to oblige."

Ryanne groaned when the baby executed an impromptu shuffle-ball-change. "Cowboy, it's only fair to warn you that if I don't find a rest room soon, I cannot be held responsible for what happens."

"I can help there, too."

"I doubt it." Ryanne pressed her hands to the small of her back. A cloud skidded past the full moon, permitting a quick glimpse of her rescuer's face. Too tanned to be a vampire. Way too amused to be dangerous.

That was the good thing about podunk towns. They didn't have much to offer psycho ax-murderers.

"Well, don't just stand there." She knew some might call her tone "bitchy," but she preferred a less-common adjective such as *churlish*.

"What is it you expect me to do?"

"I don't know. Rob me? Mug me? Dump my battered body in a bar ditch?" Like a stressed-out lab rat, Ryanne could no longer run the maze. Biting the head off her own kind seemed a logical progression. "Is that what you're planning?"

"Hell, no, ma'am."

"If you have crime on your mind, I can save you the trouble. Nothing I own is worth working up a sweat over."

"Ma'am, I don't want anything."

"What? You're just a good-ol'-boy Samaritan? Have spitty hanky, will travel. Is that it?"

"Something like that."

"Okay, then. Watch my stuff while I go to the bushes. And it better be here when I get back or I will track you down and sit on that silly hat."

"But I—"

"Just watch it, buster." Although what he had to

guard it against, she had no idea. A marauding coyote perhaps?

"Yes, ma'am."

Ryanne picked her way into the darkness, muttering to herself. She threw a parting comment over her shoulder. "And stop calling me ma'am."

"Yes, ma'am."

She thought of bugs and snakes only in passing. She was more worried about the man in black, a gifted quipster who communicated only in short sentences. There was something unnervingly familiar about him. Or maybe the unnerving part was knowing he waited, politely, on the other side of the shrubbery while she conducted business of a very personal nature.

And she thought the world had run out of ways to humiliate her.

Tom Hunnicutt wasn't interested in the woman's pile of battered, mismatched suitcases. But like a man who couldn't tear his gaze away from a train wreck, he was fascinated by the woman. Despite the bad attitude, the lopsided ponytail, and the gummy bare feet, she was just about the cutest little egg-shaped female he'd ever seen. Even if she did waddle like a Christmas goose.

Who was she? What was she doing here? And why had she been put off the bus in the middle of the night? Those were all legitimate questions, but what he really wanted to know was, how did such a tiny girl carry around a belly like that? She had to be expecting a medium-size third-grader.

"Do you have a phone, cowboy?" Miss Congeniality was back and she had a way of making even simple questions sound like stamp-her-foot demands.

"Yes, ma'am."

"Didn't I tell you to stop ma'aming me?" She thrust out her hand.

Not knowing what else to do, Tom shook it. "Nice to meet you. I'm—"

She snatched it back and propped it on her hip. "May I *use* your phone?"

"I don't have it on me. It's attached to the house."

Using an I-must-be-speaking-to-the-impaired voice, she drew a vague circle in the air. "Is...there... a...phone...any...where...around...here?"

Tom didn't much appreciate the implied slur on his intellect. He was only trying to assist someone who obviously needed all the help she could get. However, even good-old-boy Samaritans had limits. He wasn't a robber or a mugger. And he was no clabberheaded fool. But if the little mama wanted dumb, he could give her dumb.

He shuffled his feet. "Ah, shucks, ma'am. Nearly ever' body in Brushy Creek's gotta telly-phone nowadays. They got the e-lectric, too." He doffed his hat and scratched his head in broad hayseed fashion. "'Cept ol' Possum Corn back in the hills. He don't hold for nothin' fancy as all that."

Her pretty face wrinkled in a pained grimace. "Oh, no. I've gone and offended you. I am *so* sorry."

Such total lack of sincerity. "You run around loaded for bear like that, a fella's bound to get grizzly."

She took a deep breath. "I really am sorry. It's just been—"

"Let me guess. A rough day?"

"Actually it's been a rough year, but why nitpick over the details? Can we start over? I'm Ryanne Rieger."

He stepped forward for a closer look. "I don't believe it. *You're* little Ryanne?"

She patted the small mountain that was her belly. "Not so little these days, but, yep, that's me."

"Birdie said Short Stack was coming home." Her foster daughter's fall from grace had been a hot topic with the coffee and pie crowd at Mrs. Hedgepath's diner.

"No one's called me Short Stack since I waited tables at the Perch. You know Birdie?"

"Place like this, everybody knows everybody."

"And everybody's business, I suppose?"

"Pretty much."

She made another face. "So what else do you know?"

"Birdie might have mentioned your, uh, difficulties. In passing."

She threw up her hands. "Oh, great. Please tell me the whole dang populace doesn't know that my marriage *and* my career have been sucked down the toilet."

Tom fought a smile. She sure had a way of turning a phrase. "Possum Corn, back in the hills, might not have heard. He doesn't have a telly-phone."

"Very funny."

"There was one thing Birdie left out."

"My shoe size?"

He looked pointedly at her expanding middle. "She didn't say a word about you being in the family way. That was a big surprise."

"*Big* being the operative word."

Tom frowned at the unmistakable waver in her voice. One minute she was fit to be tied and the next she was teetering on the brink of tears. Her mood swings might not make *her* dizzy, but they sure did him.

"Do you remember me?" he asked. "I'm Tom Hunnicutt."

She stood on tiptoe and pushed his hat back with her

finger. A cowboy didn't tolerate many people messing with his headgear, but he'd overlook it this time.

Her eyes widened. "Omigosh! Tom Hunnicutt? No wonder you looked familiar. I used to have such a crush on you."

"You did?" The unexpected confession should not have surprised him. Ryanne seemed to blurt out whatever thought her brain sent tongue-ward.

"Please. Me and every other girl in town. I was so stuck on you, I wanted to propose when your team won the college rodeo championship."

"Why didn't you?" The dog-bitten scrap of ego he had left was duly flattered.

"I was grounded because of my math grade. Birdie said anybody who couldn't do decimals, couldn't get married. Even to a hotshot saddle bronc rider."

He laughed. Maybe Ryanne wasn't unstable after all. Her flightiness could be a temporary condition brought on by stress. "It's just as well. What were you, ten?"

"Twelve. And you were already engaged. A fact that caused no end of bitter disappointment among the adolescent female population, as I recall."

"I don't know about that." He was unaware of mass adulation, adolescent or otherwise. As long as he could remember, there had been only one love in his life.

"You had a childhood sweetheart. What was her name?"

"Mariclare Turner." He couldn't say her name without tasting the regret. He'd lost the woman he loved because he'd assumed his dreams were enough for her. It never occurred to him she might have dreams of her own.

"Oh, yeah. Mariclare-with-the-Perfect-Hair. That's

what we jealous teens called her. You're still rodeoing, right?"

"No. I'm not." Realizing how harsh that sounded, he added, "I got hurt last summer and had to give it up."

"Sorry to hear that."

It was bad manners to stare, but Tom had never been this close to anyone so busting-out pregnant and didn't quite know where to look. He chose down. Bare feet seemed a safe alternative to protruding belly button and excessive cleavage. Ryanne was shaped like a primitive fertility totem he'd once seen in a museum, and that made him nervous.

"Does your daddy still own the store?" She stood with one foot propped on the instep of the other. Her feet were far from humongous. They were tiny. Fragile. The bones in the one he'd held had felt as insubstantial as a child's. Hardly strong enough to support her weight.

"Yeah. Pap had a quadruple bypass last winter and it slowed him down some, but he's hanging in there." He held up the key to Hunnicutt Farm and Ranch Supply. "I could have let you in to use the rest room."

She rolled her eyes. "Now you tell me."

"I tried. You wouldn't give me a chance. That was some kind of roll you were on."

She failed in her attempt to look abashed. "I know. My mouth always gets me in trouble. Birdie says it'll be the first part to wear out. Forgive me?"

It was hard not to. She had an exasperating charm. Her blinding, 100-watt smile was calculated to make a man forget how high-strung she was. "We'll chalk it up to duress."

"Hey! Maybe I could use the phone in the store to call Birdie. She would have met me, but she's not expecting me until next week."

He frowned. "It's after midnight. No sense in her driving all the way into town. I'll take you home."

"Really? That would be great. If you're sure you don't mind trekking out to the boonies in the middle of the night."

"I'm running behind on good deeds this week." Tom quickly committed to the plan. The sooner he handed Ryanne over to Birdie's safekeeping, the sooner he could get back to what passed as his life these days. He scooped up the suitcases and directed her across the street to a black late-model, extended-cab pickup. He tossed the bags in the back while she climbed into the front seat.

"There's been some zoning changes since you left," he said as the engine purred to life. "Officially, Birdie doesn't live in the boonies anymore. She's out in the sticks, ten miles farther down the road."

Chapter Two

The truck's headlights detected little movement as Tom drove out of town. An occasional larcenous raccoon was the only night-life in Brushy Creek. The beer joint locked up at ten o'clock during the week because good farmers went to bed with the chickens. Even the convenience store closed at nine.

"Must feel good to sit down." He was still trying to figure out the logistics of carrying that belly around.

"Yeah. Haven't done much of *that* lately."

"The bus?" He decided *pert* best described her features. *Disheveled* summed up her appearance. Her personality was pure spunk with generous helpings of sass and vinegar.

She shuddered dramatically. "Have you ever ridden a bus?"

"Just to school when I was a kid."

"Oh, no. That doesn't even begin to count."

He stole another glance. Despite her tart tongue and bossy manner, she looked incredibly young and vulnerable. The thought of her making a long trip alone aroused feelings he'd forgotten he had. Protective feelings. When was the last time he'd been tempted to reach out to a woman? And why was he so tempted by this little bouncing ball of trouble?

Before long they were riding through rolling hills. The Department of Tourism called this northeastern corner of the state "Green Country." Tom had traveled extensively on the rodeo circuit, all over the west and north to Canada. He'd seen a lot of fine country, but always figured someday he'd settle down in Oklahoma, close to his roots.

In his big-money days, he'd bought eighty acres of prime grazing land a few miles south of town. There was a pretty, wooded knoll on the property, and he'd dreamed of building a log home on top of it. One of those sprawling, lodge-pine jobs like he'd seen in Colorado. He thought it would be the perfect home for Mariclare. For their children.

Besides kids and dogs, he planned to raise and train horses. Turn his acreage into a tidy little quarter horse operation. Someday.

He never quite pinned it down, but *someday* was always that time in the vague future when he'd made enough winning rides. When he'd worked the rodeo out of his system. When he could retire from the circuit and never look back.

He'd learned the hard way that it was a mistake to put dreams on hold. They had a short shelf life. He'd postponed until everything was gone. Rodeo. Mariclare. Kids. All of it. Maybe he *was* a clabberheaded fool. He should have seen it coming. She'd begged him to quit and he'd kept riding.

Since he was unwilling to choose real life over rodeo,

a wild-eyed bucker had chosen for him. Ten charmed years with no injuries more serious than sprains and scrapes, and he'd ended his career with a bang.

A concussion, two compound fractures, and three broken vertebrae. Multiple surgeries to repair the damage. Weeks in rehab. Months of casts and canes. Bottles of pills for the pain and inevitable depression.

It had taken a year, but he finally looked whole on the outside. Inside, something vital had been severed. And that wound wasn't even close to scabbing over.

"I'd forgotten how far it is to Birdie's." Ryanne was not as comfortable with quiet as the strong, silent cowboy beside her. He watched the deserted road like a freeway at rush hour.

"As they say around here. It's a 'fur piece.'"

Light from the truck's space shuttle instrument panel cast a greenish glow over his face. She'd been eleven the last time she'd seen Tom Hunnicutt. It was in the café, the day he left for New Mexico State on a rodeo scholarship. He'd been excited. His parents had been proud. Heck, the whole town had been proud. Local boy makes good.

He'd been a lanky, smooth-cheeked teenager then. Now a mature thirty, he'd finally grown into his masculinity. Strong chin, straight nose. Couldn't beat a combination like that. She couldn't see his eyes, but recalled that they were so dark pupil and iris were one color. A boyish dimple and a crooked grin wrapped up a very appealing package.

She might be eight months pregnant, but she wasn't quite brain dead. Or body dead, for that matter. Her pheromone receptors were alive and well and capable of going on full red alert. But she'd made a decision during the grueling bus ride. She didn't need another man in her life. She needed to learn how to enjoy being alone. All urgent twinges would henceforth be ignored. They were nothing but trouble.

Giving in to twinges, urgent and otherwise, was what had set her on the fast track to disaster. It would pay to remember that.

"What were you doing in town so late?" she asked.

"I was driving back from Tulsa. When I saw the bus pull out and you standing there all alone, I thought I should do something."

"Do you always brake for damsels in distress?"

"No," he admitted. "But you seemed to be in a bit more distress than most of the damsels I run into."

And he had a killer smile. Which she would also ignore along with all ensuing twinges. She sighed. Good thing she was *enceinte* and he had The Clairol Girl.

The truck hit a hole in the road and bounced Ryanne's head to the top of the cab. "Ow!" Startled by her yelp, Tom slammed the brake and she pitched forward.

"Jeez, Louise!"

"Are you all right? I didn't see that pothole."

And she thought he was watching the road. She grasped her belly with both hands. "Are you prepared to midwife, cowboy?"

"You mean you're—?"

"No, I'm not in labor. Just don't hit any more of those craters." She frowned at his queasy expression. Big, strong men were so squirrelly about childbirth. "Good thing males don't bear children or the human race would be extinct."

"If men had babies," he said as he accelerated, "we'd have figured out a better way to do it by now."

She laughed at his serious tone. "Something less time consuming, perhaps?"

"And not so messy."

"You have strong opinions. Which are based, I assume, on your extensive experience with..."

"Dogs and horses."

The truck rounded a curve and trapped a deer in its headlights. The animal froze in the classic pose and Tom tapped the brakes to give it time to gather its wits and leap into the underbrush.

"It's been a long time since I saw a deer in the road," she said quietly. It gave her hope that the world was not such a bad place, after all.

"So tell me about Nashville," he said. "I was in town the summer after you left and I remember Pap moaning about how his favorite waitress had lit out to make a big splash in the country music business."

"You know what they say about best-laid plans," she muttered.

"What is it you do again?"

Maybe it was unreasonable, but the question hurt her feelings. And was just a smidge irritating. In a town where everyone knew everyone and their business, evidently her life was of little consequence.

"I play the fiddle and sing." She tried not to sound as defensive as she felt. "And write songs."

"So did you make a big splash?"

Ryanne rubbed her belly. "Not really. I neglected to check to see if the pool was filled before I jumped in."

"Half-cocked."

"I beg your pardon?"

"Pap said something about you tearing off half-cocked."

"Remind me to thank *Pap* for the vote of confidence." She knew very well that impulsiveness was her downfall. Hell, half-cocked was her modus operandi.

"Don't take it personally. He just hated to lose a good waitress."

"Being a waitress, even a good one, was never my primary career goal. However, the way things are going, I can't rule it out."

"You didn't have any luck in Nashville?"

"Luck is relative. If they paid musicians to audition, I'd be rich. Actually, I got pretty close a few times."

"Real close from the looks of you."

"I was referring to breaks." It came out as cool as she intended. She didn't need the local cowboy to remind her that if she'd concentrated on her music and ignored those pheromone twinges, she wouldn't be in her current predicament.

"Mmm-hmm. I see."

"What do you see? A big fat pregnant failure running home like a whipped pup?" Ryanne's anger swung out of left field, surprising even her. But he'd blundered into sensitive territory, and she needed to use the damned bushes again.

"I figured you came home to be with Birdie." He looked concerned. "For the baby."

The tears came fast and hard. Six terrible months, capped off by two horrible days, finally caught up with her. "Never mind that I'm broke, or that my husband deserted me."

Ryanne gripped the seat. Uh-oh. She was in for another ride on the old estrogen roller coaster. "Did Birdie mention I got fired because itty-bitty cocktail waitress outfits don't look perky on pregnant ladies?" Sniff. "Or that I got kicked out of my room because I was three months in arrears? Or that the bank repossessed my car out from under me? I guess what you see is, if it weren't for Birdie taking me in, I'd have to whelp in the street like a stray dog.''

Ryanne ended on a high, damp note. She hated crying. It was not her style to wallow in self-pity or inflict her troubles on others. Damn the hormones that jerked her around like a mindless puppet.

Tom took the sandblasting in silence, his strong profile set in stone. She should be ashamed of herself. She'd really unloaded both barrels this time. And on a poor cowboy trying to do a good deed.

But, Lord, it felt good.

Tom drove quietly during the minitirade. What kind of loose cannon had Ryanne Rieger turned out to be? Mood swings were one thing, but he wanted no part of her emotional excess.

The louder she got, the tenser he became until his jaw ached and he white-knuckled the steering wheel. It had been a year since a woman had yelled at him like that. He had not missed the experience one damn bit.

Ryanne sniffed some more and wiped her leaky eyes and nose with the back of her hand. "So now you know. I'm a failure. Down and out and knocked up."

Tom kept his eyes on the road. He didn't want to career through any more potholes, and he didn't want to look at the girl weeping beside him. As long as he didn't, she was just a noisy distraction. He didn't want to glance over there, and see some wrung-out kid who needed him to make her feel better. He was out of the feel-good business.

"You're not a failure." He didn't mean to sound gruff.

"I didn't do what I set out to do. I'm divorced, broke, homeless. Last I looked, that wasn't a recipe for success."

"You tried, didn't you? Failure is not trying. So your dreams didn't come true. Get over it. Then try again."

She leaned back and folded her arms over her belly. "I am in no mood for sensible advice."

"You'll survive. You're the feistiest little pregnant lady I ever met."

She succumbed to mirthless laughter. "Oh, brother. What a thing to say. Feisty little pregnant lady? Damn!"

"Maybe you can start a club." Tom watched the road, worried she might go off on another crying jag.

But the next time she laughed, it was real. "Or a twelve-step program."

"There you go." He let out a slow breath.

"Hey, that gives me an idea for a song. 'I ain't got nothin' left but spunk/ but I can't get far on that.' What do you think?"

Tom smiled in the darkness. Good thing she had a sense of humor; she'd need it. He made the mistake of looking at her. Her wide eyes reminded him of the frightened doe.

Damn. He didn't need this. And he didn't want it. "It" smelled too much like involvement.

"Or how about this? 'I don't have a husband/ I don't have a home/ but I'm gonna have a baby/ so I won't be alone.'"

"Sounds almost pitiful enough to be a hit." He found it hard to resist her ability to act up, even when she was down.

"You think?"

"It'd be better if your dog died. Or you maybe drove an eighteen-wheeler."

"I'll work on it."

He turned to her after a few minutes. "Feeling better?"

"Yeah. I'd forgotten how good it feels to have someone to talk to."

Yeah, right. If she wanted a sympathetic ear, she was barking up the wrong cowboy. According to Mariclare's exit speech, he was incapable of listening. Too wrapped up in himself to care about others. What was it she'd called him?

Oh, yeah. An emotionally unavailable, self-centered SOB.

The accusations had cut deep. He'd had a lot of time to think about them. He knew she had her reasons, but he could never quite reconcile the heartless man she'd described with the one whose face he shaved every morning.

Tom stuffed those feelings down and concentrated on maneuvering the curves. Ryanne was humming now. Like she was testing out an elusive melody heard only in her head. She'd been through a lot for someone so young. He didn't want to add to her pain.

And he did not want to share it.

"I don't know what happened to me back there," she said. "It was either a fleeting episode of temporary insanity or a really bad case of bus lag."

"I reckon you just needed to let off steam."

"You reckon?" She laid her head back on the seat. "Just don't think I'm a high-strung, world-class hysteric. I'm not. Normally I'm pathologically stoic."

She made it sound like she cared about his opinion. He wasn't sure how he felt about that. "You'll be home soon."

"Home. You don't know what that means to me."

But he did. He'd come home to lick his wounds, too. To find comfort in the familiar world of his childhood. To slip back into the skin of the nice guy he'd once been. The man he'd been when he left Brushy Creek. The one his hometown thought he was. "Home is the place you can't appreciate until you leave."

"That's pretty poetic for a cowboy." For once she sounded sincere.

At least she'd calmed down. He wasn't up to handling raw emotional upheaval in any form. With his own future so uncertain, he sure as hell didn't want to get involved in anyone else's life right now.

Especially not the overwrought, messed-up life of an abandoned fiddle-playing wannabe country singer who looked like she could give birth and/or have a nervous breakdown at any moment.

In his heart, that hollow place he'd boarded over when Mariclare walked out, Tom knew Ryanne needed reassurance that things would be all right. But understanding the problem and taking responsibility for it were two different things.

No way would he volunteer for any comforting jobs. He had enough problems, without letting some little gal get under his skin.

Ryanne let out a sudden squeaky yelp.

He resigned himself to another outburst. "Now what?"

She grinned and patted her belly. "Tom Hunnicutt, meet the future clogdancing champion of the world."

Chapter Three

Birdie Hedgepath's house on Persimmon Hill crouched among tall post oaks and pines at the end of a long gravel drive. A pole light between the house and barn illuminated a weedy yard where leggy petunias spilled from old tires.

Everything was just as Ryanne remembered. Peeling white paint on the clapboards. Plaster hen and chicks under the crape myrtle bush. Pink plastic flamingos clustered around the propane tank.

The old porch swing stirred in the breeze and the creak of its rusty chains brought a rush of memories. Hot summer days. Cold Pepsi. Shelling beans. Birdie and meaning-of-life discussions.

Nothing had changed. Insects filled the night with their noisy chorus. Down at Annie's Pond the bullfrogs belted out the amphibian top ten. Even Froggy, Birdie's rheumy-eyed old hound, was in his spot by the door. He barely looked up at the midnight intruders.

Ryanne took a deep breath. She'd missed the smell of

this beautiful green place. She'd been so self-absorbed that for five years she hadn't thought once about barn owls or little sulfur butterflies. She'd forgotten the feel of dew-damp grass on bare feet. The sound of bobolinks.

In her single-minded pursuit of fame and recognition, she'd discounted the treasures left behind. She'd worried that coming home meant moving backward instead of forward. That embracing the past meant giving up on the future.

She was wrong. Persimmon Hill wasn't the end of the road. It was a place to rest while she repaired the damage of her own foolish choices. Her life might be going to hell in a handbasket, but here she would be safe.

Home was the most sentimental song of all.

Tom set the last of the bags on the porch. "No one answered?"

"I haven't knocked," she admitted. "I'm just taking it all in."

"Let's surprise her." He didn't know what had gone wrong in Ryanne's life, but when he saw the look in her eyes, he knew she'd been right to come here. He motioned her back into the shadows behind him. He rapped, and in a moment a sleepy-eyed woman in her midsixties pushed open the screen door.

Birdie Hedgepath's quarter Cherokee blood showed in her round face, high cheekbones and dark eyes. She and her late husband Swimmer had no children of their own. If she hadn't taken in ten-year-old Ryanne when her mother died, the child would have become a ward of the court, and sent to live among strangers.

Birdie did not possess the frailty her name implied. She had substance. Shoulders that were wide for a woman. A waist and hips to match. Stout legs, flat feet. Her black hair was cut short and streaked with gray.

Though strong physically, her real strength was her wisdom and humor. Everyone who met Birdie, loved her.

"Landsakes, Tom," she said with a yawn. "What're you doin' out here this time of night?"

"I brought you a little something I picked up in town." He stepped aside with a dramatic flourish.

"Oh, oh, oh! You brung my baby home." She pressed her hands to her mouth then threw her arms wide. "Baby girl, come here to me and let me hug your neck."

"I missed you, Auntie Birdie." Ryanne's eyes filled with damp happiness. "I don't know why I stayed away so long. I'm glad to be home."

"Not half as glad as me. Let me look at you. Ohwee, girl, have you gone and swallowed a watermelon seed?"

"Something like that." Ryanne gave her foster mother another hug. "You smell exactly as I remember. Like lilacs and bacon."

Birdie's dark-eyed gaze raked Ryanne from her cock-eyed ponytail down to her bare feet. "What did you do, Tom? Drag her backward through the brush all the way?"

Ryanne laughed and hugged her again. "It's a long story."

"And one I aim to hear. Tom, you get those bags in the house and I'll put on some coffee. Probably got a pie around here somewheres."

He carried the luggage inside, but declined the offer. Like a messenger delivering a prize, he had no right to hang around and enjoy it.

"Thank you, ma'am, but I need to get home. I know you two have a lot of catching up to do."

"You go on then. But stop by the Perch and I'll wrap up one of them blackberry cobblers you and Junior favor so."

"Thanks. I'll do that. Birdie. Ryanne." He tipped his hat and stepped out into the night.

Ryanne caught up with him as he climbed back in the pickup. "Thanks again for hauling me out here. I'm sorry about, well, you know. Getting all weird earlier. It's the hormones. Normally I'm a much nicer person than what you've seen tonight."

Tom felt an inexplicable urge to touch the spirited woman and claim some of her energy for himself. He settled for a light tap on the tip of her nose. "Nothing wrong with the person I saw."

"Good night, then." She stepped away from the truck, but seemed reluctant to let him go.

Or maybe he was just reluctant to leave. "Good night, Short Stack. Take care of the little dancer."

When the rooster crowed, Ryanne and Birdie were still at the kitchen table. It had taken hours to catch up. Since nothing ever changed in Brushy Creek, Ryanne had done most of the talking.

She chose to edit out the sordid details of her brief marriage. What Birdie didn't know wouldn't hurt her as much as the truth. So she took pains to keep her voice light as she described what she hoped sounded like a run-of-the-mill marry-in-haste, repent-at-leisure scenario.

They talked about the baby, and Birdie offered emotional and financial support. Then she insisted on making biscuits and eggs before driving to town to open the café. It was Friday morning, and there would be a crowd of regulars waiting for her breakfast specials.

"I'll go with you." Ryanne cleared the table. "I want to earn my keep and you know I'm a whiz-bang waitress."

Birdie, who had changed into her uniform of white polyester slacks and tunic, bent to tie her athletic shoes. "You had a good teacher, didn't you? No, honey, you stay here. You need to rest. Take a warm bath, then go straight to bed. You hear me?"

"Yes'm. I *am* tired."

The older woman gave her another measuring look. "Tired? You look like you've been sortin' wildcats."

"I know. I'm a mess." Ryanne cleared the table and set the dishes in the sink.

Birdie kissed her cheek. "But you're my mess and I'm glad to have you."

"I can't imagine what Tom thought." She ran dishwater into the sink. "He probably went home and told his wife all about the wild-eyed maniac he picked up at the bus stop."

Birdie looked up, her broad features puzzled. "Wife? Why, Tom ain't never been married."

He hadn't wed his too-perfect sweetheart? It seemed she'd made the wrong assumption. "What about Mariclare Turner? I thought those two would be married by now."

"Nope." Birdie shook her head. "She up and left him a year ago. It hurt him bad, her running out on him that way. I don't know the whole story, but Junior said she left while Tom was in the hospital after that bronc stomped him."

"But they were engaged for as long as I can remember."

"Since high school," Birdie confirmed. She swigged the last of her coffee and set the cup on the counter. "You could have knocked me over with a feather when they split up. It's funny he didn't mention it."

Ryanne squirted liquid soap into the dishwater. "He's not the chattiest guy I ever met."

Birdie nodded. "I've known a lot of rodeo hands in my time. They're tough and they keep a short rein on their feelings. They don't talk about problems."

Ryanne cringed when she recalled how she'd spilled her guts the night before. He surely thought she was a flake.

"Cowboys have to ride, no matter what," Birdie went on. "They learn to ignore physical pain. They get so used to aching, they ignore it when the hurt's on the inside, too."

"That doesn't sound very healthy."

Birdie gave her a pointed look. "And climbing on a thousand pounds of bucking horseflesh does?"

"I see what you mean." She put the dishes in the sink.

"When Tom first came home, he was all broken up. Mind, body and spirit. He had a right to grieve."

"I'm guessing he didn't," Ryanne said.

Birdie frowned. "He shoved his sorrow down to the bottom of his heart and pretended it didn't exist. First time I saw him after he came back, he looked like the light of his soul had sputtered out. Everybody knew he was hurtin,' but he wouldn't talk about it or let anybody help."

"Tom's strong."

"And stubborn," Birdie added. "You know, you might be good for him."

She smiled. She'd forgotten how much Birdie liked to "fix" things. And people. "How so?"

"Tom needs to get on with his life, and you're about as full of life as anybody I know."

"I can't get involved with anyone right now, Auntie."

"What? You can't be friends with a man who needs one so badly?" the older woman asked with exaggerated innocence.

Ryanne could use a few friends herself. She'd been alone long enough to know it wasn't a natural state for her. But she wasn't in the market for a man. If the time ever came when she was, she planned to take things slow and easy. No more rushing into things. She knew, all too well, the consequences of falling in love too fast.

"Well?" Birdie prodded.

"'Friends' sounds good." In a way she was glad that Mariclare-with-the-Perfect-Hair hadn't turned out to be the quintessential sweetheart. If couples who'd known each other all their lives couldn't stay together, how could lightning-strike courtships like hers be expected to succeed? She felt so much better about her own problems she actually hummed as she washed the dishes.

"Ryanne?" Birdie's expression was as amused as her tone.

"Yes, ma'am?"

"Did you hear what I said?"

"I'm sorry. I must have spaced out for a bit."

The older woman grinned. "That's okay, honey. You go right ahead and think about him all you want."

Ryanne hid her embarrassment by scrubbing a coffee mug that was already clean. "What do you mean?"

"Never mind." Birdie separated a key from her key ring and laid it on the table. "I was saying, drive in for supper later if you feel like it. Here's the key to the Jeep."

"No. You drive the Cherokee. I'll take the truck."

Birdie frowned. "That old beater? It doesn't have air-conditioning."

"Ol' Blue and I go way back. You taught me how to

drive in her, remember? I want to take her out for old times' sake.''

"You sure?''

At her nod, Birdie shrugged and handed her another key.

"Auntie Birdie? Are you going to warn people about me?'' Ryanne asked softly.

"What for? You going to bite them or something?''

"You know what I mean.'' She patted her belly. According to Tom, Birdie hadn't mentioned her pregnancy. She'd never say so, but maybe she disapproved.

Birdie gave her a reassuring hug. "My baby's going to have a baby. If you want anybody to know more than that, you can tell them yourself. I'm busy in that café, you know. I don't have time for gossip.''

Right. Ryanne watched the Jeep disappear down the dusty road. Brushy Creek didn't have a newspaper or a radio station. It had Birdie's Perch. That's where everyone headed when they wanted information. Or a darn good piece of pie.

Ryanne washed her hair, gave herself a facial and polished her nails. Then she soaked in a tub of bubbles until all the nagging aches eased from her body. The little dancer, as Tom had called her, cooperated fully and allowed her to sleep eight straight hours in her old bed.

She woke up feeling refreshed, like maybe she hadn't lost her grip after all. As she dressed for supper she wondered if Tom would stop by the café. Did she want to see him? The fact he was unattached didn't change anything. Or did it?

The answer was definitely no. She had enough on her plate right now. She needed a man in her life like a frog needed spit curls. She would stomp and squash any twinge that dared to rear its hormoney head. Never again would she let runaway emotions rule her life. From here on out, caution would be her middle name.

Hopefully, there was truth to the old adage "once burned, twice learned." Having been thoroughly toasted on the altar of matrimony, she should be a blooming genius.

Still, there was no denying the unsettling current of excitement she'd felt when Tom touched her last night. It was just a casual tap on the nose, but it had jolted her like a poke from an electric cattle prod. Her shameless reaction was probably no more than a leftover from her girlhood crush. Like all leftovers, it couldn't possibly taste as good the second time around.

Maybe she wasn't trying to impress Tom or anyone else, but Ryanne took extra care with her makeup and hair. She was tired of looking like day-old road kill. Old friends would stop by the Perch for supper, curious to see how the world had treated her. She didn't want to look like something set on the curb for immediate disposal.

At this stage in her pregnancy it required sleight of hand to appear even moderately fashionable, so she chose the one dress that had not been designed by a Bedouin tentmaker. The beige crinkled-cotton number floated around her bulky figure and showed her shoulders to advantage.

She added a silver choker and dangly silver earrings to draw attention away from her midsection. Much like trying to camouflage an elephant with a hairbow. She slipped into a pair of leather mules that didn't pinch her feet, and checked the results in the full-length mirror.

Not bad for a fat lady.

She wasn't returning from a triumphant engagement at the Grand Ole Opry, but she had her pride. She was no longer a sad little orphan. And she wasn't Short Stack, the Teenage Waitress. She was about to be a mother. She might not have much to show for the past five years, but she had gained maturity, worldliness and poise.

Well, not worldliness. That would be a stretch. Maybe not poise. But definitely maturity. She'd aged ten years in the last five.

She climbed into Ol' Blue and cranked the key a few times before the engine roared to obnoxious life. Just like the good old days. She guessed Birdie had last used the truck to haul cow manure for the garden. As it rattled down the drive, backfiring all the way, bits of dried dung swirled around in the bed and blew out to litter the road.

Did she know how to make an entrance or what?

Tom locked the front door of Hunnicutt Farm and Ranch Supply behind the last customer of the day. It had been six months since he arrived to give Pap a hand, and he was getting antsy.

Junior Hunnicutt, always vigorous, had bounced back from heart surgery sooner than expected. Maybe one of these days Tom would work up the courage to tell him his son didn't plan on following in his retail footsteps. Not that there was anything wrong with selling feed and fertilizer. It was just that the job required too much time indoors.

The store's long-time success depended on skills Tom simply didn't possess. He was no chip off the old salt block when it came to such things as anticipating trends, creative stocking and inventory control. Or shooting the breeze with customers—what Pap called public relations.

"I'm going over to Letha's for supper tonight, son."
Junior flicked off lights. "I won't be late."

"That's the third time this week. I think the widow
Applegate is testing the theory that the shortest way to
a man's heart is through his stomach."

"You ought to taste her chicken and dumplings.
Mmm-mmm." Junior smacked his lips. A widower for
four years, he was a food lover from way back. He'd
lost weight since his illness, but his pearl-snapped Western shirt still strained around his apple-shaped torso.

Tom grinned. He was glad his father had found someone as nice as Letha Applegate. At least one of the Hunnicutt men could get on with his life. "Home-cooked
meals usually have strings attached. I'll leave the dump-
ling tasting to silver foxes like you."

Junior placed the cash drawer in the old-fashioned
safe in his office. "You're a young man, son. There's
other fish in the sea. Other women in the world."

Tom, who was a full head taller than Junior, grasped
him gently by the shoulders. "I love you, Pap. But have
you ever heard the expression, 'don't go there'?"

"Yeah. What's that mean, anyhow?"

"It's a nice way of saying butt out." He wouldn't talk
about what happened between him and Mariclare. There
was no need. It was over. Done with. End of story.

"You shouldn't keep everything bottled up," Junior
said with studied empathy. "You need to share your
pain."

"And you need to stop watching so many talk
shows." Tom flipped off the portable TV set, silencing
a talk-show hostess in midsentence.

Junior shook his head. "I worry about you, Tommy."

"Don't. I'm fine."

"Are you sure you can manage on your own tonight?"

"I'll survive." Ever since he'd been home, his old man had been killing him with kindness. Junior was recuperating from open-heart surgery, but he acted as though Tom was the fragile one. Hell, a *broken* heart wasn't life threatening.

"You could stop by the Perch for supper," his father prompted.

"I might." Tom wondered if Ryanne was the reason there were so many cars on Main Street. Something had brought people into town, and it wasn't just the best chicken-fried steak in the county.

Pap had an annoying habit of reading his mind. "If you see Short Stack, give her my regards, will you?"

Tom walked down the street, noting the filled parking spaces. The café would be crowded, and he'd have to wait for a stool at the counter. Unlike the rest of the town, he was interested in eating, not gawking at Ryanne.

So why not go somewhere else? There were other places to eat. He pushed open the café door, and a bell announced his arrival. Because those places didn't serve Birdie's special blackberry cobbler, that's why.

Ryanne was holding court in a corner booth in the back, surrounded by people she hadn't seen for years. They inquired about her health, but what they really wanted to know was had she met Shania Twain or Travis Tritt. Thankfully, they were well mannered enough not to mention her lack of Grammys. Or her divorced and expectant status.

When the bell jangled, Ryanne looked up and saw Tom Hunnicutt—for the first time in bright light. Wow.

Bus haze and semidarkness had definitely minimized the full hunkiness effect. Now that she had recovered and he was properly illuminated, it hit her.

Like a wet sandbag upside the head.

This was the man who'd rescued her from a blob of evil bubble gum? The man who'd witnessed her various and assorted tantrums? The man she'd shanghaied aboard the estrogen roller coaster? The talk around her faded to a hum when the tall cowboy doffed his black hat and winked in her direction. He stepped up to the counter and spoke to Birdie, propping one booted foot on the rail.

That was the set of taut manly buns that had pressed up against her?

Like the blinking neon sign in the window, a whole new wave of twinges perked up and demanded notice. Ryanne tried to pay attention to the conversation, but it was useless.

Apparently she'd been rendered temporarily deaf.

Tom had been a sweet-faced boy. He gave adolescent girls heart palpitations without making their daddies too nervous. He'd changed. Now he was a man capable of throwing grown women into full-blown cardiac arrest.

His black-and-white-striped Western shirt fairly glowed in the fluorescent light. His boots shone like mirrors, and his black Wranglers sported razor creases and a fancy belt buckle.

The faint fan of wrinkles at the corners of his black opal eyes were an unnecessary, but appealing embellishment. His hair was thick and dark, combed back from a wide forehead and creased by his hatband. He smiled at something Birdie said, and a dimple in his left cheek came out to play.

The dimple alone was guaranteed to increase the anxiety level of daddies everywhere.

"Evening." Tom acknowledged those around the table, but didn't really see them. He was so entranced by Ryanne's transformation he couldn't see anyone but her. "You clean up pretty good."

"Thanks." She stuck one slender leg out from under the table and dangled a tan leather mule from her toes. "Shoes and everything."

"Half of one, anyway," Tom teased. "You look so different, I might not have recognized you if I met you on a dark street again."

Ryanne laughed as she related the details of their first meeting. Somehow she made the story of Tom's rescue sound far more amusing than she'd considered it at the time.

"Tom here is a regular knight in shining Stetson," she concluded to nods of agreement.

The men in the group slapped his back before returning to their tables. The women smiled. One old lady actually reached up and pinched his cheek.

"You always were such a *nice* boy, Tom," she said as she tottered off.

"Is that true?" Ryanne scooted over in the round booth and motioned for him to join her.

"Is what true?" It was hard to concentrate. Maybe he *had* spent too much time in closed places. He certainly felt confused and light-headed as he folded his long frame into the worn seat.

"What Mamie Hackler just said about you always being a *nice* boy."

"I hate to contradict a sweet old lady, but she doesn't know everything."

Tom couldn't get over it. The tearful, bedraggled girl was gone. In her place was a lovely young woman who radiated charm and confidence. Her dark hair was pulled back in a froth of curls, her green eyes sparked with humor. Unlike last night's edgy ragamuffin, this woman would be right at home on a stage, soaking up the adoration she deserved.

Last night he'd convinced himself she was nothing but trouble. He should stay as far away from her as small-town living allowed. But Ryanne Rieger was a hard woman to forget. Working around the store today, he'd found himself thinking about her and the circumstances that had brought her back to Brushy Creek.

She leaned close and whispered. "Birdie's thrilled about the business, but I can't believe all these people came by just to see me."

He kept his tone light as he inhaled the languid, peachy musk scent of her perfume. "You're the most exciting thing to happen around here since a family of skunks set up housekeeping under Bidwell's Drugstore."

"Thanks a heap." She dumped sugar into her iced tea.

Her throaty laugh bubbled up like an artesian spring. How could a man tire of hearing that sound? He was about to ask about her ex-husband when Birdie brought their food.

The chicken-fried steaks hung over the edge of the plates, accompanied by cratered mounds of mashed potatoes and gravy, and string beans seasoned with ham. The meal was served with tossed salads and thick ranch dressing, freshly baked rolls, and cucumber and onion relish.

"Can I get you anything else?" The older woman put her hands on her hips and beamed at them.

"How about someone to help me eat this?" Ryanne teased.

"You're eatin' for two, young lady. Tom, watch her now, and make sure she doesn't pick."

"My pleasure." Not that he could tear his eyes away from her if he tried.

They kept to small talk while they ate. The waitress refilled their glasses, and Birdie peeked out of the kitchen from time to time, seemingly satisfied that Tom was doing his job.

Ryanne had eaten less than half her food when she put down her fork. "I'll pay for this later with the worst heartburn known to womankind, but it was worth it."

"Birdie's the best cook in the county," he agreed.

"Do you come here often?"

"Pap and I are pretty useless in the kitchen." He forked another bite of steak into his mouth.

"Birdie told me your mother passed away a few years ago. I was sorry to hear it."

He accepted her condolences. "Pap sends his regards, by the way. He has a lady friend now, and he's having supper with her tonight."

"Why, that sly old dog." She set her plate aside and folded her arms on the table.

She leaned toward him, and he got another head-turning whiff of her perfume. "I'm just glad to get him out of the house," he said. "Pap thinks me staying in my old room makes me fourteen years old again."

"All parents worry about their children. Especially their only children. I'm glad to hear Junior takes the job seriously." She poked an errant strand of hair back into the pile on her head.

Tom was distracted by the movement of her silver earrings. He noticed her waiting expectantly, but had no idea what she'd just said.

"How long have you been back?" she prompted.

"Six months. I came to help him after the surgery, but now he's making noises about retiring. He's mentioned that I should take over the store so he can spend time at the lake."

"And?"

"I don't think I'm cut out for shopkeeping. I might go back to scouting stock."

"What does that involve?" She sipped her tea.

"When I got out of the hospital, I worked for a stock contractor in Texas, making the rounds of ranches, checking out bucking horses for sale."

"Like a baseball scout, looking over the home teams?"

"In a way. Some have tried, but you can't really breed a bucking horse. You have to find him." He drank the last of the tall tumbler of tea. It was his second refill, so why was his mouth so dry?

"I never thought about where they came from."

"They're valuable animals. A top bronc can bring up to $15,000. Contractors won't let loose that kind of cash unless they know they're getting their money's worth."

"And you know horses."

"Yeah." His knowledge of horseflesh was the only thing he was sure about these days.

"Do you recall the day you left for college?" she asked. "You and your parents came in here for lunch."

The question caught him off guard. He couldn't reconcile vague memories of a shy little girl playing waitress, with the grown-up Ryanne. "You expect me to remember something that happened twelve years ago?"

"I do," she confessed. "I took your order. You had a barbecue beef sandwich with fries and coleslaw. And a root beer. I think."

He shook his head in amazement. "I can't believe you remember that."

"I told you, I had it bad for you back then."

She shrugged and he gazed at the expanse of pale skin stretching over her collarbone. It looked so soft. He could see the tiny blue veins beneath it. He had an unnerving impulse to trace that fine network of veins with his finger.

"I had no idea." He shoved the impulse aside. It took all his concentration to keep up with the conversation.

"That you were the first boy I didn't want to lob spit balls at?"

Tom laughed. "That little Ryanne was a buckle bunny."

"A what?"

"Buckle bunnies are rodeo groupies."

"Cowboys have groupies?"

Tom took mock offense. "We may not be millionaire rock stars, but we have our fans."

"I guess there's no accounting for taste," she teased. "Birdie says no matter how beat-up the skillet, you can always find a lid to fit it."

Tom felt strangely at ease with Ryanne. It had been a while since he'd talked to anyone the way he talked to her.

"I remember you were a cute kid," he told her. "Trying to act grown-up with your little pencil and order book. You were actually a pretty good waitress for a munchkin."

Ryanne kicked him under the table. "I am not a munchkin. I'll have you know, I'm an inch over five feet tall. I just look shorter because at the moment I'm also five feet wide.''

The other diners cleared out by eight, closing time.

Birdie, the waitress, Tammy, and Nathan, the cook's helper, started the nightly cleanup.

Tom reached for his hat on the seat beside him. "I should get out of here." It was true, but it was the last thing he wanted to do.

Ryanne didn't understand what was happening between her and Tom Hunnicutt. But whatever it was, it throbbed like a stubbed toe and was growing harder to ignore by the minute. She liked the way he volleyed wisecracks and held his own against her jibes. She liked that he was more than muscles and dimples. He had layers. Depths.

The thought of exploring those depths filled her with anticipation.

But it didn't give her the same tingly, itchy-all-over feeling she'd experienced the first time she'd seen Josh Bryan. It was in Calico Kate's where she waited tables. He'd played bass in a band fronted by a fluffy-haired girl singer who used the microphone like a tongue depressor. The music and singer were nothing special, but Ryanne had been unable to take her eyes off the long-haired guitar player.

It had been one of those crazy things. Their gazes met. Her heart crumbled. She felt a rippling sense of danger, but knew they were meant to be together. She engineered a meeting and the inevitability of the inevitable became apparent the moment he touched her arm.

Those old voodoo pheromones in action.

What she hadn't anticipated was marrying him two weeks later, or ducking the beer bottles he tossed when he lost his temper. That fell under the heading of Unpleasant Surprise.

Never marry anyone you meet in a smoky barroom had always been sound advice.

What she felt for Tom was just as strong, but without the itch. It was totally different and definitely brain-based. Not that he didn't put her hormones on notice. It was just that in her current state, she could appreciate his more subtle charms. She could enjoy his company without worrying about all that other stuff. With him, she didn't feel compelled to play the game.

A guy like Tom probably had to fight off women with a pointy stick. No way would he be physically attracted to an out-to-there-pregnant lady. But he seemed to enjoy her company as much as she enjoyed his.

"What do you do for entertainment around here on a Friday night?" she wondered aloud.

He stood and stuffed his hands in his pockets, shuffling back into silly-hayseed mode. "I was thinking about moseying over to Odie Johnson's place to watch the corn grow."

Ryanne snapped her fingers in mock disappointment. "Darn. Given my delicate condition, I shouldn't risk that kind of excitement."

Tom's smile was puzzled. Like he was trying to decide if she was teasing or sending a signal. The fact that he couldn't tell the difference was even more endearing than the dimple.

"They'll be taking in the sidewalks soon," he said. "It's not to be missed, according to the guidebooks."

Birdie came out of the kitchen. "I'm sorry, honey. I'm going to be here awhile. The darned sink backed up and we have to clean up the mess. Why don't you go on home?"

"Can I help?"

"No. Now shoo, so Tammy can get on with her mopping."

"I can take a hint." Ryanne gave Birdie a hug before turning to Tom. "Escort me to my carriage, cowboy?"

When she tried to start Ol' Blue, the engine refused to turn over. Tom tried with the same result.

"The old girl always was temperamental," she said. "I racked up a ton of tardies my senior year."

"I could take a look at it tomorrow," he offered.

Mechanical ability *and* a dimple? "That would be great."

"Why don't I take you home? It might be a while before Birdie's ready to go."

She gave him a concerned look. "Won't that interfere with your corn watching?"

"It's a sacrifice," he admitted. "But one any good ol' boy Samaritan worth his salt would make."

Ryanne practically bounced out of the cab. "I'll tell Birdie and be right back." She lumbered toward the café, but something made her turn around. Tom had one foot propped up on the running board of the truck, his arm splayed along the open window. Looking for all the world like a buckle bunny's hottest fantasy.

It was guys like him that gave cowboys a good name.

Down, twinge, down. This meant nothing. She was just accepting another ride, and he was just being neighborly.

That's all there was to it.

She took a deep breath and waggled her fingers.

He waggled his and winked.

Don't forget, she told herself sternly. Impulsivity was *really* what killed the cat.

Chapter Four

Tom turned into Birdie's driveway, surprised that the sixteen-mile trip had passed so quickly. Small talk had come easily, as they had plenty of conversational ground to cover. They had many shared experiences despite their seven-year age difference.

They discovered they'd had some of the same teachers in high school, and skipped the same classes. They'd cheered the same losing team in the same gym and attended the same heavily chaperoned dances at the Veterans of Foreign Wars hall. Different cars and different friends, but the Saturday night streets they'd cruised had been the same.

"When I was a kid, I couldn't wait to get out," Ryanne said as he switched off the engine. "Now I realize how lucky I was to grow up here."

He knew exactly how she felt. "I've traveled all over, but I always knew I'd come back. There's something special about living in a town where people care about you."

He lifted her down from the high seat. Even with her extra passenger, she felt light in his arms.

"It's still early," she pointed out. "Do you want to stay awhile? I'll make lemonade."

"I'd like that." Tom agreed before common sense and good judgment cast negative votes. It was a mistake to stay. But leaving just didn't seem possible.

He sat at Birdie's table and watched Ryanne work. She wiggled as she squeezed lemon halves onto the knob of an antique juicer. The voluminous maternity dress billowed around her, and from the back she looked like a little girl in dress-up clothes. But she was no child. She was a woman.

A fact he was becoming increasingly aware of.

"How do you like it?" she asked over her shoulder. "Tart or sweet?"

"Tart." The word applied equally to the beverage and the woman. Now that he'd gotten used to Ryanne's style, he enjoyed her honesty. He liked her humor, her wry observations, her crazy optimism. In short, he liked her.

What was he doing? He had no business drinking her lemonade or admiring her winsome qualities. He wasn't ready to let anyone into his life. Maybe he never would be. It would take a lot to make him trust his instincts again.

"Here you go." Ryanne set a tall glass on the table. "Tart enough?"

He took a sip and grimaced, hoping to unpucker enough to answer. "Just right."

She smiled. "That's another thing we have in common. I didn't think anyone else in the world liked their lemonade as curl-your-toes sour as I do."

"Let's walk down by the pond," Ryanne suggested when they finished their drinks. "It's pretty down there this time of day. The baritone frog ensemble will be warming up for its evening performance soon."

Tom protested, but she wouldn't take no for an answer. "Oh, come on, I need the exercise. Do you want me to lose my girlish figure," she teased as she tugged him through the weedy yard.

"Be careful now. Those shoes weren't designed for off-roading." He took her hand as they crossed the pasture behind the house, helping her through the tall grass. If the tense expression on his face was any indication, he didn't enjoy the contact nearly as much as she did.

They walked down to the shady, spring-fed pool the locals called Annie's Pond. No one remembered the legendary Annie who, distraught over unrequited love, had flung herself into its shadowy depths. Ryanne said the story was romantic, but scoffed at any woman doing herself in over a man.

"You cynic. Don't you believe in true love?" Tom helped her lower her bulky self onto a flat rock.

"I used to. I'm not sure anymore." She leaned back on her palms. The stone held the sun's heat, and its warmth relaxed her. Overhead, oak and persimmon leaves rustled in the breeze. A bobolink called in the distance.

"Jimmy Tench and I used to sit out here," she said. A lifetime had passed since those carefree high school days. Once upon a time, when her dreams were new.

Tom folded his long legs and sat in the grass beside her. "For a little tonsil hockey perhaps?"

"Nothing like that. Jimmy and I were buds." The poor boy had been forced to listen to, but not allowed to challenge, her lofty plans. They were confidants, and she'd helped him over some rough patches, as well. She realized with a start that she'd rather go through life without a lover than without a friend who believed in her. She didn't believe one person could fill both roles.

"We came here to talk," she said. "Jimmy had a lot to work through after his father left."

"It's rare for someone who claims her mouth is her worst enemy to also be a good listener." Tom picked up a flat pebble and skipped it across the still water.

"Nice arm." She pitched one across the pond. It skimmed four times before dropping beneath the surface.

Tom nodded appreciatively. "Very impressive."

"Jimmy taught me that." She gazed at the far side where tall cattails grew. Dragonflies darted among the lily pads, and their iridescent wings glinted in the waning sunlight. "You got a scholarship to college. Did you graduate?"

"Yep. I got a degree in ranch management." He chewed on a long blade of grass. "But I wasn't much of a student. All I cared about was the rodeo."

"All *I* ever cared about was music." For once in her life Ryanne exercised restraint by not asking questions about his broken engagement. If Birdie was right about the cowboy code, Tom wouldn't appreciate her getting personal. With effort maybe she could force the conversational ball into his court.

Crickets, cicadas and frogs all felt free to fill the silence, but not Tom. Since she couldn't stand dead air, she jump-started things by asking him why he took up bronc riding.

He shrugged. "I was good at it."

"I'm good at dishwashing, but I don't want to do it for a living."

"You have an answer for everything, don't you?"

"If I did, I wouldn't have to ask."

"I liked the adrenaline rush of the ride."

"What about fame and fortune?"

"Rodeoing's not about that. It just gets in a man's blood and he's hooked."

"Like an addiction?" The sun had slipped behind the trees, casting his face in shadow. But she didn't think that was the only reason his expression darkened.

"No. More like a craving that can only be satisfied by going to the next show."

"'He loved his damned old rodeo.' At least that's what Garth says."

"You either love it or you hate it. It's a sport like no other. Cowboys don't have managers. They don't hold out for more money. In fact, they have to pay to compete. There's no guaranteed salary, no contracts. Just man versus animal."

"Sounds romantic."

He placed his hat on his knee and raked his fingers through his hair. She thought he had the softest-looking hair she'd ever seen on a man.

"If your idea of romance is getting the tar pounded out of you on a regular basis," he said with a sharp laugh.

The heat and buzzing insects made Ryanne drowsy after the heavy meal. She was always tired these days. "I'd like to know how you got hurt. If you want to tell me."

Tom watched the dragonflies dip and hover like tiny helicopters on a rescue mission. Maybe it *was* time to talk to someone. He knew every gory detail of the disastrous ride, having watched the videotape dozens of times. Forward. Backward. In slow motion and freeze-frame. But he hadn't discussed it. Not with Pap or Mariclare, and certainly not with a therapist who was paid to listen to people whine.

Pap wanted him to share his pain. He couldn't do that, but hell, maybe it was time to start letting some of it go.

"It happened last summer. At the West of Pecos Rodeo in Texas," he said quietly. "I drew a good horse. Hellbender had a reputation as a crowhopping gravedigger, but I was ready for him. It should have been a winning ride."

"What happened?"

"I lost my concentration in the chute. I nodded, the gate opened, and I woke up in traction. I got bucked off, but my boot hung up in the stirrup and Hellbender did a Mexican hat dance on me."

Ryanne shuddered at the chilling image, and he had a sudden urge to smooth her furrowed brow. "How bad was it?"

Tom recited the laundry list of injuries. Concussion. A broken arm and leg. Cracked ribs and vertebrae. Bruised kidney and ruptured spleen. "There weren't too many square inches on me that weren't black-and-blue. That firebreather messed me up good, but it was my fault."

"If it hadn't happened, would you still be riding?"

"I don't know," he said honestly. Would he have quit? Could he have walked away from the sport he craved to make the woman he loved happy? He was only thirty years old, but sometimes he feared the best part of his life was over. "Rodeoing is for the young and limber."

"You're still young," she pointed out.

"Only in years, Short Stack. Only in years."

Ryanne reached for his hand and placed it on her belly

without any apparent thought for the intimacy of her action. "Do you feel that?"

Long moments passed before he felt the tiny bump beneath his palm. "What is it?"

"She has the hiccups. There she goes again."

Something stirred in Tom. Touching Ryanne felt too good to be right. It would be so easy to pull her into his arms. To kiss her busy mouth. Too easy. He withdrew his hand, regretting for a moment that the quickening child did not belong to him. But it wasn't fair to ask a new life to give meaning to his.

"I didn't know they got hiccups in there." He had no words to voice the awe he felt. Or the confusion.

"Oh, yeah. She does it all the time." Ryanne stroked her belly as though caressing her child, and his own skin ached for her touch.

"You keep saying 'her.' Do you know for sure?" He hoped it was a girl. A little angel, as bright and high-spirited as her mother. The sad old world sorely needed more spunk.

"Just intuition. I couldn't afford the ultrasound to determine the sex."

"It's a wondrous thing, isn't it?" It was hard for him to comprehend that a tiny human being rested beneath her mounded belly. Sleeping. Stirring. Waiting to make its entrance into the world.

"It's a miracle," she agreed.

Ryanne's sweet smile affected Tom like an embrace, filling him with a rush of powerful emotion that quickly turned to resentment. He'd been so careful to protect his heart the past twelve months. How could he let a girl he'd known less than twenty-four hours tangle him up in knots?

He had to keep up his guard around her. She was little.

She looked harmless. But without a doubt, Ryanne Rieger was one of the most dangerous women he'd ever met.

They sat quietly while shadows fell. Annie's Pond grew dark and mysterious. From time to time a catfish surfaced to gulp an unsuspecting insect. Fireflies flashed in the gloom.

Ryanne hadn't known such peace in months. Problems could not intrude here. Maybe Birdie was right. Maybe things would work out. There had to be a reason the soap opera of her life had followed this particular script. Hope for the future began to trickle back into her heart. This was where she belonged.

But was it the place she found so reassuring? Or was it the man beside her? Lulled by a longed-for sense of security, she impetuously voiced her thoughts.

"I feel comfortable here with you, Tom. I feel like I've known you forever."

He glanced up, surprise lighting his dark eyes. "We go back a ways. If you count the adolescent crush thing."

"I just don't want to get involved." She picked a blade of grass and shredded it. "Romantically."

"I understand." His whole body appeared to tense, and she wondered if maybe she'd been *too* honest. He probably hadn't even thought of her in a romantic way.

"I don't want, or need, to hook up with anyone at this point in my life," she explained with a nervous shrug.

"I understand." He said it again, but he didn't look as if he understood. He looked like a man trying to decipher a code. Or translate an ancient language.

A bullfrog leaped onto a lily pad and ribbited its two cents worth into the conversation.

"You and I have a lot in common," she pointed out. Like her, Tom had been betrayed by someone he loved. He, too, had come home looking for solace. Between them, they'd written the book on disappointment.

"What, we've seen the elephant?" he asked wryly.

"Exactly. We're like veterans. We didn't fight the same battle, but we share the battle fatigue. I know what you've been through because I've been through it, too."

"What do you know about what I've been through?"

Uh-oh, there was definite frost in his tone. As usual, she'd crossed the line and put him on the defensive.

"Just what's in the public domain," she assured him. "You said it yourself. In a place like Brushy Creek—"

"Everybody knows everybody's business."

"Exactly." She thought about her conversation with Birdie. "I don't need a relationship, but I could use a friend. I think you could use one, too."

"I doubt we've been acquainted long enough for you to know what I need." He flung another pebble into the water.

She wouldn't let a few ruffled feathers stop her. "Oh, don't get all bent out of shape. You could obviously have any woman you want. I figure if you *needed* a physical relationship you'd have had one by now."

"What makes you think I haven't?" His dark eyes narrowed.

"Oh, please. You haven't had time. And you're not that kind of guy."

"What kind of guy is that?"

"The kind who blindly jumps into things. Jeez, you were engaged for, what, twenty years?"

"Only twelve."

"Only twelve. Mr. Impulsive."

"So how long were you engaged?" He cocked one dark brow.

She was never one to ignore a challenge. "Josh Bryan and I got married two weeks after we met." Tom looked as horrified as she'd known he would. "It was one of those crazy, spur-of-the-moment things that seem like a good idea at the time," she hastened to assure him.

"You knew some guy two weeks before you married him?"

"Yeah." Ryanne should have anticipated his reaction. Any man engaged to his childhood sweetheart for twelve years would have trouble with the concept of whirlwind courtship.

"God, Ryanne. That's crazy." He plowed through his hair again. "Downright irresponsible. How could you do something like that?"

Her shrug was eloquent. "We fell in love."

"What happened?" His tone demanded an answer.

"We fell out?" she offered sheepishly.

"Don't be flip, Ryanne," he chastised. "Things are never that simple. What about the baby? What kind of man runs out on his pregnant wife?"

"One who doesn't know?" She winced, anticipating his reaction to her latest revelation.

"What?" His face clouded with disbelief.

"Josh left before I found out. We had a fight. He shoved me around and—"

"He hit you?"

"Calm down, cowboy. He'd been drinking. He was upset because he lost out on a job he wanted. Did I mention he's a musician? He plays bass."

"That's no excuse." He folded his arms across his chest.

"The bass playing?"

"No, the drinking."

"I agree." Given his cowboy code of honor, Ryanne suspected Tom could make no exceptions for brute behavior. That was one of the things she liked about him. "Anyway, he left. He claimed his luck had changed for the worse since he met me. He said he'd never get anywhere in the business while I was around. I believe the term *albatross* was bandied about."

Tom's disapproval was obvious. "That makes no sense."

"I know. What do seabirds have to do with anything? But never try to reason with a drunk whose mind is made up."

"I don't believe this. He's a drunk, too?"

"Oh, not chronic. Just when the occasion demands. He must have sobered up pretty fast because two weeks later I was served with divorce papers."

"How long were you married?"

"Six months. It seemed longer, though," she said as an afterthought.

"And you never saw him again?"

"Only when he came to pack his stuff. He brought three husky friends along so I wouldn't overpower him and make him stay." She'd given up all hope for a reconciliation when she realized Josh couldn't see her without adequate backup.

"So when did you find out about the baby?" Tom was having trouble following the sequence of events.

"A month later. I used four of those home pregnancy tests because I refused to believe the little plus signs. Surprise, surprise."

"I don't understand. Why didn't you tell him about the baby when you found out?"

"Oh, right. Josh considered a wife an albatross. Do you *reckon* he'd be a big fan of fatherhood?"

Tom ventured a guess. "No?"

"A big definite no. That's why I'm giving the single mother gig a try."

"And took your maiden name back when you divorced?"

"Never changed it. Can you imagine being Ryanne Bryan?"

"It could be worse. I know a Ruby Luby." Tom walked down to the water's edge. Fireflies flickered around him, and the bullfrog flopped back into the water. "It's getting dark," he said without turning around. "Maybe we should head back to the house."

"So what do you think?" Ryanne asked his back. She tried to stand up but couldn't work up enough leverage to become bipedal on her own.

"About what? You threw a lot at me there."

"About us being friends. If you don't give me a hand up, I'll have to camp out on this darn rock until I give birth."

He turned to face her. "Only you would think friendship is something that has to be negotiated." His words sounded as tight as her underwear felt.

"I think it's best to define parameters. That way, there are no unfulfilled expectations. I read somewhere that unfulfilled expectations are the single most damaging thing in any type of relationship."

"Is that a fact?" He gave her another of his dark looks.

"Yep." She had had morning sickness for three solid months. And not just in the morning, either. It would take more than one of Tom Hunnicutt's grizzly-bear glowers to intimidate her.

"And?"

"And if we're up-front with each other and agree that all we expect is the emotional support of platonic friendship, we can avoid problems later."

He shook his head as if trying to clear the confusion. "Are you always like this?"

"Like what?"

"So outspoken?" He made it sound like a cross between gifted and perverse.

Her smile let him know she wasn't insulted. "I find it saves time." She waggled her hand at him, and he ignored it.

"I see. So what you're saying is, you don't find me attractive."

"Don't be silly. You're a total hunk. I just don't want a girl/guy relationship right now." And the twinges he caused were merely meaningless artifacts of her first girlhood crush. Irrelevant holdovers. Nothing to worry about.

"Girl/guy?" The corners of his mouth edged up in a reluctant smile.

"You know what I mean. I need to get my act together. I have to stand on my own, and figure out what I want to do with my life. Jeez, I'm gonna be somebody's mother in a month. I have important things to do. I can't be distracted by a bunch of mushy stuff."

Once Tom started laughing, he couldn't seem to stop. He doubled over from the effort.

"What's so darn funny?" she demanded.

"You. I think Birdie's right. Your mouth *is* going to wear out first."

"I'm just being realistic." She flapped her hand imperiously until he finally pulled her up. How could she stand on her own two feet when she couldn't even get off her backside without help? She dusted the back of her skirt, totally discounting the way her heart leaped at his touch.

Friends don't let friends feel twinges.

"That's all well and good. But what happens later,"

he asked, "if, hypothetically speaking, one of us wants more?"

She hadn't planned that far ahead. "You mean like years down the road?"

"Okay," he said with poorly concealed amusement. "Years." He made a rolling gesture with his hand. "Down the road."

"We'd discuss it." She brightened. For a minute there she thought her plan had backfired. She didn't want him to wiggle out, fearing she'd renege on the deal and cramp his style.

"Renegotiate the terms?" he asked skeptically.

"Reevaluate expectations."

"That's the craziest thing I ever heard." He laughed at her disappointed look. "But I must be crazy, because it almost sounds doable."

She indicated her enormous belly. "I know you can't be interested in me physically, because I'm such a blimp I should have Goodyear printed on my side. I'm impulsive and emotional and unstable. Not at all what you need in a woman."

"You seem to have strong opinions on what I need."

"You'll find I'm pretty opinionated."

"Pretty, anyway."

She ignored his lame attempt at a compliment. She knew exactly how *not* pretty she looked. "We'd be a terrible couple. But as friends we can give each other balance. You can reel me in when I go off the deep end. Help me be more steady and cautious. On the other hand, I can teach you to loosen up, be spontaneous."

"I take it you've given this a lot of thought?"

She couldn't tell him that she and Birdie had actually discussed it. That might seem like a conspiracy. "Actually, it sort of just came to me."

"Ooh, like a vision?" He acted like a phony hypnotist, complete with spooky sound effects.

He could make fun of her if he wanted. She was on another roll, and she wouldn't back down now. "Let's call it a revelation. The whispering of a higher power."

"So it really is as hare-brained as it sounds?"

"Totally," she agreed with a grin. "What do you say?"

He eyed her doubtfully. "I don't know. Do I have to sign a contract or anything?"

She punched his arm. "You're kidding, right?"

"Ow." He massaged the injured area. "It was a spontaneous attempt to loosen up."

"Well, it needs work." She stuck out her hand for the obligatory sealed-deal handshake. What a relief. She needed a friend. Not a lover. She could have Tom in her life without messing it up with something as sticky as falling in love.

She was an accomplished messer-upper.

"Deal?" she prodded.

Tom held her hand for a moment after he shook it. He had a knowing look in his dark eyes. A look that said he believed they'd made a fool's bargain. And he knew she knew it, too.

Too darn bad. He could stare into her heart till the cows came home. Nothing would make her admit their agreement had definite Faustian overtones.

"Deal." Tom's smile was one of capitulation. "Far be it from me to argue with fate or the complicated logic of Ryanne Rieger."

Chapter Five

The next day Tom performed his first official act as Ryanne's new "best friend." Resuscitating the ancient pickup truck she was so fond of. She watched like a kid at a magic show as he adjusted the alternator belt, cleaned the crusty battery terminals and connected the jumper cables.

Wiping his hands on an ever-present red bandanna, he leaned around the open hood. "Get in and give it a crank."

When she turned the key, the asthmatic engine coughed to life. Giving the steering wheel a gleeful thunk, she climbed down from the cab.

"Oh, thank you, Doctor Cowboy." She clutched her hands to her ostensibly pounding heart. "You're a lifesaver. Or should I say, trucksaver? Birdie threatened Ol' Blue with the junk heap if she had to pour any more money into her."

Ryanne's enthusiasm had a leavening effect on Tom.

Making her happy, even in such small matters, made him feel better about himself. "It's just a temporary fix."

He removed the cables, and assumed the serious demeanor of a cardiac surgeon with bad news to break. "I'm afraid Ol' Blue's gonna need a battery transplant."

Aside from her undying appreciation, Tom's mechanical sleight of hand earned him a free meat loaf lunch at the Perch. In typical steamroller fashion, Ryanne had quickly settled in as the rush-and-relief waitress, backup table busser, and alternate counter wiper.

He stopped by the café every day. Sometimes for a hurried burger lunch, sometimes a leisurely supper with Pap. Even if she was in a back booth catching up on bookkeeping chores Birdie had gotten behind with, Ryanne nudged the regular waitress aside with a smile and served his food herself. Claimed she had to "keep her hand in," in case it became necessary to resume waiting tables full-time.

If she weren't needed elsewhere, she leaned on the counter to chat. Keeping to light conversation, she marked time by tapping her foot to an internal rhythm. She hummed melodies while she worked, frequently trying them out on his untrained ear. Sometimes she pulled out her order book and shared lyrics she'd scribbled in a rush. Tom was flattered that she valued his opinion of her work.

Ryanne was in perpetual entertainment mode, a master at customer relations, who made all who walked in the door feel special. She lavished friendly smiles on everyone, but Tom wanted to believe the ones she saved for him were different.

On Thursday morning of the second week, Pap sent him to the Perch on an emergency sweet-roll-and-coffee run. The breakfast rush over, there was only one other customer at the counter.

"Morning, Tub." Tom slid onto a stool next to an appropriately dubbed local and gave Tammy his order. Two black coffees and a cinnamon roll to go.

Ryanne popped out of the kitchen, wearing a silky green maternity top and white pants cropped off below the knee. Pulled back by a tortoise-shell headband, her dark mane floated around her shoulders. "Hey, cowboy."

"Hey, you. You're not working today." She rarely bothered with makeup, but today she'd blushed her cheeks and artfully accented her eyes and lips. She looked so lovely his heart actually thumped in response. He'd heard expectant mothers had a special glow about them, but Ryanne wore the luminosity like the aura of an angel.

She made a Betty Boopish primp. "Nope. I'm wearing my going-to-towns today. I got places to go, people to see."

He knew he was grinning like a moon-eyed fool, but he just couldn't stop staring at her. She was such a startling contradiction of fragility and strength. Tough, without being hard. Vulnerable, but far from weak. A pure mystery inside a confounding puzzle.

As he considered that, he was smacked in the gut by the powerful urge to bend her over the bar stool and kiss all the lipstick off her rose-colored mouth.

Shocked by his unseemly thoughts, he clasped his hands on the counter to keep them harmlessly occupied. Where had that come from? Why did she suddenly affect him in such an inappropriate way? He had to be a lech to have thoughts like that about a trusting little pregnant woman. Especially one who'd picked him for her Friend of the Month Club.

That's what came from reading too much into a smile. Or in having second, third, even fourth thoughts about the outlandish bargain they'd struck.

Maybe it was nothing more than the shock of seeing her out of "uniform." Today's getup was a far cry from the usual plain white T-shirt and stretchy jeans, worn under an apron with an embroidered birdhouse and ties lengthened with ribbon to span her burgeoning middle.

Setting Tub's waffles and sausage in the window with a crisp "Order up," Birdie stepped through the swinging doors. She peeked with disapproval into the paper sack Tammy had set on the counter in front of Tom.

"Why don't you take two of them cinnamon rolls?" she asked. "I baked 'em this morning and they're melt-in-your-mouth fresh."

"I'm sure they are, Birdie, but coffee's all I want and Pap's on short rations. He's not supposed to clog up his new arteries. Doctor's orders."

"Humph." Tub Carver lit into his breakfast with one sympathetic, monosyllabic comment.

Birdie placed Tom's money in the cash register, closing the drawer with her hip. "Ryanne, honey, you'd better get a move on. You don't want to be late."

"Where're you off to?" Tom pocketed the change, striving for what he hoped was casual, *friendly,* interest. Inquiring minds just wanted to know.

Birdie answered for her. "She's going to Claremore to see the doctor."

"Is anything wrong?" Broadsided by visions of vague, yet potentially life-threatening prenatal complications, he sounded anything by casual.

"Yeah, something *is* wrong." Ryanne hitched up her belly with mock woe. "I can't seem to find my toes."

"She's just going in for a checkup," Birdie assured him. "She got an obstetrician to agree to take care of her for the duration and tend to the delivery."

"You're not taking Ol' Blue, I hope." He'd jolted the old truck back to a semblance of life, but it was far from roadworthy.

"Birdie's making me take the Jeep." Ryanne rolled her eyes as though driving the shiny SUV would cut into her fun.

"Tom, I tried like the dickens to get her to ask you to drive her over there." Birdie gave Ryanne a pointed look. "But the bigger around she gets, the stubborner she becomes."

The expression Birdie turned on Tom was the equivalent of a poke in the ribs. She had to dangle the bait a moment before he caught on enough to bite.

"Why don't I drive you, Ryanne?" He tried to make it sound like a why-the-heck-didn't-I-think-of-that idea. But in light of the indecent kissing urge he'd just suppressed, the prospect of spending several hours alone with an attractive female with whom he was supposed to observe strict platonic parameters was a daunting one.

"Thanks, cowboy, but that won't be necessary." Ryanne pulled her child-size purse from under the counter and set the strap on her shoulder. "I've lost my waspish waistline, not my ability to operate a motor vehicle."

"Tom don't mind driving you, hon. Why, he jumped at the chance like a hound on a pork chop." Birdie's dry assertion underscored Tom's obvious physical and mental quandary.

Ryanne turned to him and sighed. "There are times

when you just have to overlook the elderly's unfortunate lapses in judgment.''

Birdie let that one pass and refilled Tub Carver's coffee cup. "She's got no business taking off cross-country by herself.''

Tub obviously felt obliged to weigh in with a carefully considered opinion. "Nope.''

"Sheesh. I'm not setting out to explore the Outback. Claremore's only thirty highway miles away.''

"And Lord only knows what could happen between here and there.'' The older woman was apparently the only one who fully understood the danger inherent in the risky undertaking.

"Birdie, please.'' Ryanne turned to Tom. "Stop sweating. I won't ask you to give up the better part of your day.''

"I don't mind. Really.'' What would she think if he admitted the better part of any day was the part he spent with her?

"Thanks, but between you hauling me out to the Hill and fixing Ol' Blue, I've probably used up all the favors our short acquaintance entitles me to.''

"Hogwash. What are *friends* for?'' His emphasis wasn't exactly a jab, but it definitely tweaked. Judging by Ryanne's tight-lipped reply, she got the message.

"You're generous to offer, but we kinda put you on the spot there.'' She flung an accusing look at Birdie, the guilty "we'' in question, and eased toward the door.

"Not a problem.'' Tom's enthusiasm for the project grew in direct proportion to Ryanne's perceived discomfort. He wouldn't let her squirm out of this one. It served her right for wanting to control everything. For thinking she could orchestrate a relationship the way she composed music. A real friendship should just happen. The terms shouldn't have to be outlined in advance and shaken on, like a car deal at the bank.

It was easy for her to stay inside the box in a busy café. Why not spend the day together and put it to a real test? The more he thought about it, the more Tom liked the idea. Maybe she'd blurted out that whole "we've seen the elephant" speech because she didn't trust herself to keep her hands off him without the security of rigid guidelines.

"I couldn't impose." She was halfway to the door.

"Matter of fact, Pap asked me to drive over there on store business, anyway." He informed not only Ryanne, but also Birdie, Tammy and Tub, who were now fully vested in the drama. "I was going tomorrow, but I reckon I could kill two birds with one tank of gas."

"You reckon? I'd hate to interfere with business." Ryanne's crisp demurral was a jab back at him. She continued backing along her escape route.

The suspense was apparently killing Tub who mopped up maple syrup with a last bite of waffle and popped it into his mouth. "They going, or not?"

"Of course, they're going." Birdie rounded on them like a border collie with two wandering lambs and propelled them out the door. "And just so my hardheaded darlin' don't crumble under the burden of debt, Tom and Junior can have all the free cobbler they can eat until the baby comes."

"I don't know about that, Birdie," Tub said as he sipped his coffee. "The way Junior likes pie, he might bankrupt your whole operation."

Ryanne watched Tom run into the farm-and-ranch store to drop off Junior's midmorning snack and pick up the newspaper ad layouts due at the Claremore Daily

Record. When he came out, he set the truck's powerful air conditioner on the polar-ice-cap setting and tuned the radio to a country station.

"So you really do have business in Claremore?" she asked as they pulled onto the two-lane highway.

He patted the ads in the folder on the seat between them. "Yep."

"Be that as it may, you didn't have to do this." As much as she enjoyed Tom's company, she chafed at the notion of always being a good deed needing his attention. How could he respect her if she was constantly begging favors? Back at the diner, she'd sensed his reluctance at being sucked farther into the black hole that was her life, which only made her more determined to refuse his offer.

He accelerated around a slow-moving tractor. "Like I said, I don't mind."

The farmer on the tractor hiked his forefinger on the steering wheel, rural sign language for "have a nice day." She wished Tom would just stop protesting how much he didn't *mind,* and say he actually wanted to be here.

"Well, it was wrong of Birdie to take advantage," she said, "just because you're a nice guy."

"I'm not *that* nice. So stop apologizing."

"Just so you realize, *I* know you were coerced."

"Duly noted."

"Fine." She felt an unreasonable urge to pout, but that wouldn't enhance the mature, capable image she wanted to project.

"Fine." He stared at the road, seemingly satisfied to do what he'd been wrangled into doing.

Before many more miles had whizzed past, Ryanne felt an overwhelming need for conversation. After discussing the relative blueness of Mamie Hackler's hairdo, she tackled Tub Carver's strange weight-loss program.

"He claims he came up with it himself." He'd told her all about it that very morning. "The way it works is, each week he eliminates different foods from his diet. But here's the kicker—he does it in alphabetical order."

"So what's he up to?"

"*P*. This week, he's cutting out pizza, parsnips, pie, potatoes, parsley, pancakes and provolone cheese."

"What about Pepto-Bismol?" Tom asked with an amused glance.

"That's history. So's picnics, paprika, plantains and packages of Little Debbie Snack Cakes."

"Little Debbie doesn't start with *P*," he pointed out.

"But package does."

"I guess everyone's cranking up for the big Independence Day Festival," he said. "Is Birdie entering the chili cook-off this year?"

"Are you kidding me? Do you think she'd miss a chance to cook? It's supposed to be her day off, but she'll be up at dawn getting all her secret ingredients ready."

As far back as she could remember, Independence Day had been Ryanne's second favorite holiday, after Christmas. It was an important day in Brushy Creek, and most of the local energy went into ensuring the day's success. She'd missed the last five festivals, and was looking forward to the event this year.

They drove a few more miles, then Tom turned to her. "Tell me about your music." He seemed genuinely interested.

"You mean other than the fact that it's totally unappreciated by those in a position to appreciate it?"

"You said you came close. What happened?"

"Nashville's full of musicians trying to get a cut." He looked blank, so she explained. "Trying to find a publisher to pitch their songs to artists who might record them. Your credibility goes up once you have a cut. It's easier to attract attention. Maybe even get your own record deal. Getting a cut is like the Holy Grail of musicians."

"I guess you didn't get one."

"Nope. But I got close." She watched him ease the truck into a curve. Hands revealed a lot about a man, and Tom's were square, strong and capable. "I've chased artists down at parties, cornered them in their homes, and tackled them in shopping malls. In the humiliation department, it ranks right up there with begging on corners and standing naked before the world."

"Doesn't sound like fun."

"But it is." She warmed to her subject. "If you're a performer, you have to perform. So you seize your chances. When you're lucky you sing harmonies behind other singers or play for a luckier musician's demo. You go to open mics. Work showcases. Whatever it takes."

"A showcase sounds good."

She smiled. "Basically, it's a gig where you play for nothing so you can network with other artists and maybe some industry people. *If* you can get them to come and listen. You pin your dreams on three or four songs, sing your little heart out and hope like hell the crowd shuts up long enough for your voice to be heard. Then you pack up your guitar or fiddle and go back to waiting tables, tending bar and driving taxis. Until next time."

"I guess it helps to have a death wish."

"Said the stove-up bronc rider to the Nashville reject." Her sarcasm was thick, but good-natured.

"So what do you write about?"

She shrugged. "Love. Life. Longing. All the favored topics of those who compose music, write poems or scratch odes on the walls of public restrooms. I can only hope my point of view makes mine different."

"I'm sure you'll get another chance. You're—"

"Hardheaded?" she supplied.

"I was going to say determined. Country music has been around a long time. It'll be there when you're ready to try again."

"Yeah, but it's had a bad couple of years. Country is not as cool as it used to be."

He stopped at an intersection. "Really? Everybody I know listens to it."

"Forgive me for saying this, but duh! You're a cowboy from Oklahoma. According to people who keep score, stars aren't selling as many records as they used to. Some radio stations only play eleven songs an hour. That's down from fourteen. It makes it harder to break in."

"You say your ex-husband was a musician, too?"

"Yeah. Everything they say about misery loving company is true." The baby kicked and she massaged the spot. The tiny foot butted against her hand. Soon, darlin'. Soon.

Tom looked at her and asked, "What would he do if he knew about the baby?"

"I don't know. It's a moot question, anyway."

"Meaning?"

"I'm not planning to tell him."

He reached for the radio and adjusted the static out of Alan Jackson's "Three-Minute, Positive, Not-Too-Country Love song." He spoke without taking his eyes off the road. "Are you hiding because you're afraid of him?"

"What gave you that idea?" Her tone landed somewhere between indignant and oh, so innocent.

His what-do-you-think look didn't require an explanation.

"I am *not* afraid of Josh," she said emphatically. "And despite what you think, he's not a bad person."

"Drunks who shove their wives around don't usually win good citizenship medals," he pointed out.

"You can stop that line of thinking right there. I am not a victim, and Josh is no wife beater. It just happened that one time."

"One time too many."

She sighed. "I'm not making excuses for him. I just do not want you to think he's a total sleaze." She looked out the window and counted the brown cows and calves in a pasture near the road. Twelve.

"Why not?"

"Because then you'd think I was sleazy by association."

"I wouldn't think that." He flipped on the turn signal and turned west onto a narrow stretch of road.

"As Birdie says, I guess I didn't have the common sense to know common when I sensed it."

"Birdie's very wise."

"And Josh is very young. Responsibility scares him."

"You're young," he pointed out. "In fact, aren't you the same age?"

"Yes, and responsibility scares me, too. I never had a puppy because I was afraid I couldn't train it not to pee on the carpet. I shudder at the thought of anything cute and fuzzy depending on me."

Reaching over, he placed his hand on her belly and spoke to the mound beneath her shirt. "Cover your ears, baby, you don't want to hear this."

She didn't mean to rest her hand on his, but that's where it landed. Until he put his back on the wheel. "It's not the same thing. I fell in love with her the first time she kicked. I'm in it for the long haul."

"Did you ever consider other options?"

She didn't hesitate. "No. I don't regret my marriage. Or the child who came of it. It was bad timing is all."

"Very bad timing." His serious expression could have been concern or disapproval.

"You're not one of those old-fashioned types who believe a child needs two parents?" Hopefully, hers wouldn't require too many years of therapy to overcome its lot in life.

"Don't you?"

"In an ideal world. But parent number two is out of the picture, and that's the end of that song."

"You could tell Josh about the baby."

"Hey! Claremore—four miles." She read the road sign aloud, hoping to weasel out of replying. No such luck.

"You should tell him, Ryanne."

She shook her head. "I don't think so."

"He has a right to know. It's wrong to keep the man's child from him."

"I don't remember asking for advice in the matter." She intended her words to tease, but they came out too sharply for that.

He followed Will Rogers Boulevard into town. "Where to, Miss Daisy?"

She gave him the doctor's address and he changed lanes. "I thought, as your friend, I could give you my opinion."

"Given and taken." She noticed that traffic in the county seat had increased since her last visit.

"Maybe you're trying to punish Josh for leaving you."

"Like I'd go to that much trouble." So many new stores indicated prosperity. If focusing on the town's economic growth didn't diffuse her emotions, nothing would.

"Then you must be afraid."

"Of what?"

"That he won't care," he said quietly. "That he'll reject your daughter like he rejected you."

He waited, as though expecting her to verbally slap him back into his place. When she didn't, he continued. "Keeping quiet may be the easy way out now, but someday that little girl's gonna ask you a hard question."

"Harder than 'What is baloney made out of, Mommy?'" she asked glumly.

He wouldn't be sidetracked. "Someday your daughter will ask you why her daddy doesn't love her. Who do you think she'll blame when she finds out he doesn't even know she exists?"

"You know what, cowboy? You have an annoying habit of being insightful and sensitive at all the wrong times. Does that get on anyone else's nerves, or is it just me?"

"Aren't insight and sensitivity good qualifications for a friend?"

"You got the job based on dimple alone."

"Be serious, will you?"

She assumed an unsmiling expression, then checked her watch like a track coach. "Hurry up," she said through clenched teeth. "I don't know how long I can keep this up."

He ignored her attempt to humor him off the subject. "There's probably a psychological term for people who

use jokes to avoid the truth,'' he told her. ''I don't know
what it is, but you're a prime example.''

''Look it up under 'intimacy issues.''' She sat back,
folding her arms over her chest. She'd have to be careful
around this guy. He didn't seem much dazzled by her
self-preservation song and dance.

Tom waited for the light to change before pulling onto
the street where the medical office was located. ''Give
Josh a choice,'' he told his sullen passenger. ''Don't
make the decision for him.''

As a rule, he was no good at giving or taking advice.
He stuck to a strict mind-your-own-business policy. But
Ryanne made him want to save her from the world and
from herself.

He was moved to meddle in her life for the same
reason he agreed to her silly bargain. Except for Birdie,
she was all alone. She needed someone. A champion.
Whether by default or natural selection, it looked as if
he had the job.

Ryanne stared out the side window as though searching for the right words. When she found them, she was
as serious as a lingering case of shingles.

''Josh left me, Tom. He walked out. He got the divorce. He never came back to sift through the wreckage
or pick up the pieces. As far as I'm concerned, he gave
up the right to choose.''

''So you take the high road and give it back to him.''
He knew he was right about this. Ryanne couldn't get
on with her life if she left such an important piece of
business unfinished. He pulled into the parking lot and
switched off the engine. He didn't expect her to change
her mind on his say-so, he just wanted to make her think.

She tried to bury it under wisecracks, but there was

pain and regret in Ryanne's life that she hadn't even begun to deal with.

She slung her purse over her shoulder. "Go place your ads and come back in an hour or so."

He heaved a sigh of relief as she got out of the truck. Thank God she didn't expect him to accompany her inside. Life was complicated enough without having to face a waiting room full of estrogen-ravaged expectant mothers.

Chapter Six

Ryanne flipped the pages of a parenting magazine, her foot twitching faster as her anxiety level increased. She was in big trouble. She didn't know squat about caring for children, and in less than a month she'd have her very own child to care for. Why hadn't she taken any baby-sitting jobs when she was a teenager? That way she could have practiced on other people's kids.

But no. She'd spent her spare time slinging hash at the Perch and writing music no one would hear. This was serious. Motherhood was no part-time job she could ditch when it got complicated. Once her baby was born, she would be a mother for the rest of her life, and she had better get a clue. She scanned articles containing the latest info on colic. Breast versus bottle. Ear infections. Potty training. Age-appropriate discipline.

Jeez. How was she supposed to learn all this stuff before the little dancer made her debut? Why not take a crash course in quantum physics while she was at it?

She sighed her frustration. No amount of last minute speed reading would prepare her for the big *M*.

Motherhood. There was no way to predict the pain it would bring. No way to imagine the joy.

She tossed the magazine aside. Thoughts circled like buzzards over roadkill before alighting on her conversation with Tom. On one level she knew she was right not to tell Josh about the baby. It wasn't as if she was trying to cheat him out of anything. Just the opposite. She was letting him off the paternity hook. No way was Mr. Tight Jeans Bass Player ready for fatherhood.

But was Josh's immaturity the real reason for her silence? Tom had suggested she might have a hidden agenda. Was she guilty of keeping the baby from Josh to punish him? Of holding her unborn child hostage to her bitterness? When he left, Josh made it clear he wanted her out of his life. How could she be certain he'd feel the same about his child?

Her arms encircled her belly protectively. Tom had been right about one thing. She *was* afraid. She couldn't bear the thought of her baby not being loved enough. She knew what abandonment felt like. Her own father had left when she was barely three. There had been no child support. No weekend visits, no shared holidays, no birthday phone calls. He just walked out of her life one day and disappeared forever. She couldn't even remember what he looked like.

Rose Rieger had never quite gotten the mothering thing down and put her excessive wants and needs ahead of maternal devotion. Ryanne feared her disastrous marriage indicated a certain Rose-like lack of judgment, and she prayed every day that she had not inherited a genetic predisposition for screwing up her life.

They'd moved around a lot, usually following some

man, until for reasons known only to Rose, they had landed in Brushy Creek. Since it was time for Ryanne to start school, they'd stayed.

Along with a job waiting tables, Birdie Hedgepath had given Rose Rieger a chance. The kindly widow had taken Ryanne under her violet-scented wing, allowing her to play in a back booth during her mother's shifts. She had spent many happy hours there, coloring, playing with toys and, later, doing homework and writing down the songs that filled her head.

Birdie gave her Swimmer's old fiddle when she was eight, kindling the dreams that continued to sustain her. When she showed talent, Birdie found a teacher and paid for lessons. Rose had protested such an extravagant waste of money, but Birdie had claimed Ryanne could pay her back when she was rich and famous.

Her desire to repay the debt, and provide a comfortable old age for her benefactress had fueled Ryanne's grandiose plans, but so far Birdie hadn't seen much return on her investment. Ryanne was far from rich, more infamous than famous, and increasing her obligation by the minute.

In a karmic turn of events, Rose had died in a midnight car crash, along with the man she'd just met in a bar. Birdie stepped in with solemn efficiency, going *mano y mano* with welfare authorities who believed they knew what was best for a child they'd never met. With more maternal ferocity than Rose had been capable of, Birdie had fought to keep Ryanne close to her heart.

How could she ever repay that?

Last night, after Birdie went to bed, Ryanne had opened the suitcase of baby clothes she'd collected, mostly from thrift shops and garage sales. Sitting on the bed, she'd smoothed each tiny garment on the coverlet.

Shirts and gowns, unbelievably small. Booties. Bibs. A white dress with pink rosebuds. She'd pressed the lacy dress to her breast, praying for the strength to give her child a good life.

Lord. She wasn't ready.

Another very pregnant woman lumbered into the waiting room and lowered herself into the chair next to Ryanne. Was *she* ready? Was any woman?

Sitting in a room filled with mothers-to-be, Ryanne imagined her future self baking birthday cakes, removing training wheels, going to school programs. Attending to the countless needs of another person. It wouldn't be easy. Her own lonely mother had pretty much botched the job.

She wanted a different life for her baby. Two loving parents. A safe, secure home. Possibilities. Her baby deserved that much. *Her* baby. Hers. She felt strongly proprietary, but the child within her body was Josh's baby, too. As hard as it was for her to think like a parent, it was even harder to imagine Josh as one.

Why couldn't he be more like Tom? Dependable. Strong enough to bear the burden of the friendship she'd heaped upon him. How solidly he filled the gaps in her upside-down life. How quickly she'd come to rely on his steady presence to take her mind off her worries. The future always seemed less frightening when she imagined Tom a part of it.

Unlike Josh who couldn't think beyond his next moment on stage, Tom would be a loving, devoted father. She smiled when she thought of his big hands cradling a newborn's downy head. Of playing the fiddle while little-girl feet waltzed lightly atop his polished boots. Any child would be lucky to call Tom Hunnicutt Daddy.

And unless her pheromone reception was on the fritz,

any woman would be lucky to call him lover. Would he be sweet and gentle? Or urgent and passionate? Based on the way her hungry spirit turned toward him like a flower toward the sun, he had the potential to be either.

Or both.

She pushed those thoughts out of her mind. Not only were they inappropriate, they were very unfriend-like. Fat lot of good such dewy-eyed fantasies did her. She knew better than to trust the impulses that had betrayed her. Caving in to that insistent longing to be loved was too dangerous to risk again. She was a realist, determined not to make the same mistake twice. Unlike her mother, she did not possess an innocent, self-destructive optimism that the *next* guy would be the one.

She'd charted her course during that memorable bus ride from Nashville. She would stand alone. Put her child first. Make the necessary adjustments and/or sacrifices. That no-nonsense voice in her head would just have to shout down the whisperings of her heart.

She reached for another magazine and its cover story detailing a bitter custody battle caught her eye. Maybe what she needed was expert advice. If her ex-husband had rights to their unborn child, it was time she found out what they were. Knowledge would defuse future problems before they had a chance to blow up in her face. An attorney could explain her options, advise her in making an informed decision.

Filled with resolve, she borrowed a telephone and local directory from the receptionist. A few calls later, she found a lawyer willing to talk to her, and made an appointment for later that afternoon. She felt better when she sat back down. She had a plan. Plans were good.

She looked around. Most of the women were accompanied by partners, as today's fathers wanted to be involved in the entire experience. The presence of so many happy couples anticipating a shared event only mocked her stubborn vow to go it alone. At least she'd have Birdie's quiet strength and wisdom to see her through the birth.

If she had insisted, Tom would have sucked it up and come in with her. But how could she ask that of him? A man had to be heavily invested in a relationship before going through the challenge of childbirth.

"When are you due, hon?" asked the woman beside her.

"Three weeks. July 20." Ryanne gave the date the doctor in Nashville had projected.

"Lucky you. I still have six weeks to go. Your first?"

She nodded, and the woman continued. "My fourth."

"Wow." Ryanne couldn't imagine being responsible for four tiny, helpless humans. Was this ordinary-looking woman a superior being who had actually cracked the mommy code?

"It gets easier, you know," the stranger assured her. "It's hell the first time, because you don't know what to expect. I mean, so many things can go wrong. I was in labor twenty-four hours with my oldest. I thought I would die. Shoot, I *wanted* to die. It was the most excruciating—"

Fortunately, the medical assistant called Ryanne's name before the mother could share the grim details. The prospect of pushing a melon-sized object through a walnut-sized opening was scary enough without the horror stories of total strangers.

After the examination, the doctor instructed Ryanne to return weekly. He concurred on the due date and assured her everything was fine. The baby was in the proper position, she was young and healthy, and he could foresee no problems.

In what was obviously a rehearsed speech, he cautioned her against rushing to the hospital at the first little cramp, as she might experience false labor before the onset of the real thing.

Ryanne turned a worried gaze on the doctor. "How will I know if it's the real thing?" This was a detail she wanted to get right.

Dr. Scott patted her shoulder. "First-timers always ask that question, and I tell them all the same thing."

"Which is?"

"You'll know, dear, you'll know." He handed her a thin pamphlet of frequently asked questions, reminded her to stay active and continue taking prenatal vitamins.

Ryanne paid the receptionist with the money Birdie had given her. The doctor's vague response was more troubling than reassuring. The sharp teeth of worry gnawed at her confidence as she clutched the booklet and stepped out of the too-cool office into the blast of midday heat.

Then she saw Tom waiting in the parking lot. Leaning against his black truck with feet and arms crossed, grinning as if he was glad to see her. The frightened creatures of doubt scurried back into their holes, and she could breathe again.

After assuring him that everything was fine, she told him about her decision to speak to an attorney.

He nodded. "That's smart, Ryanne. You won't be sorry."

"The bad news is, we have a couple of hours to kill. Do you mind waiting around?"

"Not at all."

"Won't Junior be expecting you to help in the store?"

He grinned as he pulled into traffic. "I don't know why, but when I took Pap his coffee and roll, he told me to take the rest of the day off."

They decided to explore the many downtown antique stores. As they walked, Ryanne told Tom that she and Birdie had often spent the day window shopping when she was young. On Sundays when the café was closed, they came to town for a matinee, ate a pizza, then browsed the stores.

"Birdie always said, 'It don't cost nothin' to look.'" She did a fair imitation of the older woman. "We picked out all the things we would buy if we were rich, competing to see who could 'spend' the most on items we had no use for."

He laughed as they waited at the corner. "Like what?"

"Oh, red high heels. Diamond chokers. Silver tea sets. Crystal music boxes. When the salesladies offered to help us, Birdie told them we were just checking out the merchandise."

"That sounds like Birdie." He placed his hand on her back as they crossed the street.

Taking two steps for every one of his, it occurred to Ryanne that maybe her friendship with Tom was based on the same window shopping principle. As in the old days, their agreement gave her permission to covet something she didn't need, no strings attached. Was she guilty of still wanting to check out the merchandise without paying the price?

Earlier, the doctor had let her listen to her baby's heartbeat. That insistent thump, thump, thump had reminded her again of how much she wanted to give her child security. Maybe that was why she had mentally cast Tom in the father role. He was the perfect antidote to single-mom stage fright.

Or it could be those out-of-whack hormones again. For all she knew, the nesting instincts she'd read about could be responsible for fantasies as well as the urge to knit and clean closets. It'd better be a chemical imbalance. She'd vowed to take control of her life, and impulsively jumping from the matrimonial frying pan into the fire was not a proven way to do that.

Looking in the windows, Tom remarked that his mother had tossed out many of the same items, declaring them old and outdated. If only she'd hung on to the depression-era dishes and corn-shaped crockery, Pap would have had a nice little nest egg for his retirement.

Farther down the street, Ryanne paused to admire another display. It featured an exquisite antique cradle, complete with an ivory-colored comforter and gossamer canopy. The cherry wood was worn to a soft patina by the loving hands of generations of mothers.

"Wow," she said softly. "A baby would have to feel safe and loved in a bed like that."

Tom smiled down at her. "Don't worry. You'll make her feel loved even if she has to sleep in a dresser drawer."

She was still thinking about that when he thrust his arm out to keep her from walking distractedly into traffic.

"Whoa, there." His hand circled her waist, pulling her to safety.

A car whizzed by, and she stepped gratefully back into the shelter he offered. It would be easy to take advantage of Tom's strength and give herself over to his safekeeping. To live forever in the warmth of his smile. So easy.

Whatever was going on, hormonal or otherwise, she had to get a grip. There was a good reason she'd created the friend restriction, and she'd better not forget it. She had to banish daydreams in favor of platonic thoughts.

She couldn't afford the distraction of what-if, she had enough to worry about. She'd managed to assemble a matched set of problems, none of which would be solved by mooning over the handsome cowboy who'd been roped in for the ride.

"Sorry." Her heart pounded and her breath came in short gasps. Surely it was the effect of heat and exercise, and not the nearness of the man she couldn't get out of her head. "I guess I wasn't thinking."

He squeezed her shoulder. "Funny. It looked like that was exactly what you were doing."

She gazed up. The sun was behind him, backlighting his strong profile. His eyes had that softness that he seemed to reserve just for her. Her heart lurched, and she sighed again. She couldn't let herself care too much. But moments like this made it hard to remember why.

When the light changed, she stepped off the curb, hoping to outdistance the yearning of her own foolish heart. Now she recalled what she'd disliked about the shopping game.

She'd always gone home empty-handed.

Tom let Ryanne set the pace. He listened to her chatter and made appropriate responses, but his thoughts returned to a conversation he'd had earlier. After placing the ads for Pap, he'd stopped by the bank on the corner. On a whim, he'd sat across the loan manager's polished desk and asked the first tentative questions.

He wasn't ready to jump into anything, he told himself. He just wanted to get a feel for the possibilities.

The banker, a rodeo fan who'd followed Tom's career, was only too happy to discuss them. Tom told him what he had in mind, and the man punched figures into a calculator.

Tom questioned his motives as he waited for the results. Six months ago he'd come home with an ache in the place where hope used to live. He'd been hurt, angry. Disbelieving in the future because his dreams had been ground into the dusty floor of a rodeo arena, his future pounded into oblivion by flying hooves.

Laid up in the hospital, he'd thought his life was over. Then when he got too sad to face another day, he thought about his land back home. As long as he owned those eighty acres, he hadn't lost everything. They were the lifeline that kept him from drowning in a pool of self-pity. They'd been there, throughout a painful convalescence, quietly assuring him he had a reason to live.

Maybe it was time to listen. To make good on the promises he'd made himself. He could take a mortgage and build a house. Between the money he had saved and a loan from the bank, he could buy stock and make improvements necessary to get that horse farm started. He could make it happen.

A month ago he'd been ready to unload the land and take off for parts unknown. Pap didn't really need him, and the burden of pretending he hadn't failed was just too great.

Then he met Ryanne. Now he was toying with the idea of going into hock up to his eyeballs in an effort to build a future. Without even knowing it, she'd made him pull back and look at his life. The first night they met, he'd unkindly pointed out that dreams didn't always come true. He'd advised her to stop feeling sorry for herself and try again.

Try again. Could he practice what he preached?

For a rodeo cowboy, try was as important as talent, and Tom had always taken risks to get what he wanted. For years he'd ridden for the rush of those eight seconds on the back of a bucking, snorting bronc. He'd defined his life by the time he spent in the arena. Mariclare, a family, the ranch and everything else was just what he thought about while waiting for the next ride.

He'd logged thousands of miles on the road, living on greasy food, sleeping in cheesy motels, for the privilege of plunking down his entry fees and risking his life.

For what? It had all been for someday. Someday.

It was a lie he'd told so often he believed it. Now he knew better. He had ridden only for himself. Selfishness had driven him from rodeo to rodeo. Because as long as he was living from one adrenaline-pumped moment to the next, he didn't have to think about the future.

It could remain out there in the mist.

He felt guilty that everyone in Brushy Creek thought he was some kind of hero to come home and help his father in his time of need. But he knew the truth about that, too. He'd come home to hide. From the past. And from the future. The way the doctors had wired him back together, there would be no more rides.

And he didn't have anything else.

Then Ryanne happened. Without trying, she'd cracked his shell of self-indulgent suffering. The way she faced her own uncertain future made him ashamed of secretly feeling sorry for himself. She made him want to be the kind of man she thought he was.

Ryanne was his chance. He could blindly stay on the same-old regret-paved path or he could take the road less traveled. He could prove Mariclare right. Let his mistakes define the rest of his life.

Or he could redeem himself.

Ryanne and her baby made him want to get on with life. Was it crazy to want her? He'd known the "strictly friends" agreement was doomed to fail. From the moment he met her, he hadn't stopped thinking about her. She invaded his daytime musings and nighttime dreams. At first he told himself he was just concerned for her welfare. A woman alone and pregnant provoked certain feelings in all but the hardest of hearts.

But it wasn't pity he felt when he thought of her. It wasn't friendship he wanted when he imagined the way those soft tendrils of hair caressed the back of her neck. He wanted to touch her there. Kiss her there. To start in that spot and kiss his way around to that little notch at the base of her throat. He wanted to keep kissing until—

His thoughts had been interrupted by the banker wanting to share his satisfied calculations. The man had pushed the figures across the desk with a smile, assuring the doableness of what Tom had in mind.

He could build a home for her. But would she want it? Had she gotten Nashville out of her system?

"Have you browsed enough yet?" Tom sounded like a little boy who'd spent too much time at the mall.

Ryanne shrugged. "Make me a better offer."

"Would lunch do it?"

"That would just about cover it."

She chose The Rose Cottage, a turn-of-the-century home converted into a Victorian tearoom. The restaurant came by its name naturally, as the exterior was painted an eye-popping shade of pink. Tall and stately, it served as a beacon of hope in a quiche-deprived world.

Inside, the dining room was decorated in the over-wrought Victorian style, with delicate bric-a-brac, lace tablecloths, twining silk ivy, ferns and floral tableware. Recorded chamber music provided an elegant counterpoint to clinking silver and murmuring voices.

Tom glanced uneasily at the well-dressed ladies sipping tea and eating crustless sandwiches cut in fourths. "I feel like a Brahma bull in a china shop."

"You're fine." More than fine. Women were looking at Tom the way children looked at ice cream. Ryanne hardly blamed them. In dark jeans and tailored white Western shirt, he was a prize rooster in a flock of broody hens.

"I don't know why we didn't just go to the Golden Corral," he muttered as a costumed young hostess led them to a flower-adorned table by a window. "All you can eat, all the time."

"You'll love this place. It's like eating in granny's parlor."

"Yeah, that's what I was thinking." Tom pushed in her chair and perched tensely on his. He placed his hands on the table, then seemed to realize how big and rough they looked on the lace cloth, and slipped them self-consciously into his lap.

"There's so much atmosphere here," she said as she looked around.

"Can't eat atmosphere," he grumbled. "What are the chances of getting a T-bone, medium rare?" He glanced at the menu offerings. "Slim and none, I see."

"Don't be a baby. Try the Caesar salad, it's delicious."

He looked like she'd suggested the Escargot Happy Meal. "You want me to have salad? I only eat lettuce on double bacon cheeseburgers."

The smiling waitress approached with her pad, and before Tom could speak, Ryanne ordered the soup and sandwich special for two. When the plates arrived, he had the grace to look pleasantly surprised.

"Pretty good, huh?" She wasted no time digging into her lunch. The chicken and wild rice soup was delicious and so was the avocado turkey sandwich.

"Not bad," he allowed between mouthfuls.

"Admit it. It's delicious." She found his all-beef, macho cowboy attitude mildly irritating.

"Yeah, it's delicious. Just don't tell anyone you dragged me in here." His tone suggested that he found her bossy girl, told-you-so attitude slightly aggravating.

"Men," she muttered as she finished her soup.

"Women," he muttered as he polished off his sandwich.

After lunch, Tom drove Ryanne to the attorney's office. He offered to go in with her, but she assured him it was a task best done alone.

"You don't have to do everything yourself, Short Stack. It's okay to lay down the load once in a while."

She placed her hand on his arm. "Thanks. But—"

"How about I go find some manly activity to occupy my time?" he said with a grin.

"If you don't mind." She opened the door and picked up her purse. "Damn!"

"What's wrong?"

"I forgot. I gave all the money to the doctor. I don't have anything left for the lawyer. What was I thinking?"

Tom tipped to one side and pulled his wallet out of his hip pocket. Opening it, he counted five crisp twenties into her hand. "Give him that as a retainer. He can bill the rest."

She pushed the money back at him, refusing to give in to grateful tears. "I can't take this. How will I ever pay you back?'' Stand alone, indeed. She was nothing but one big, needy charity case.

He clutched the steering wheel so she couldn't put the money in his hand. ''Go on, get out of here. You'll be late for your appointment.''

Ryanne explained her situation to the young lawyer, Gordon Pryor. He folded his hands on his desk. ''Is there any chance of a reconciliation between you and your ex-husband?''

''No.''

''You answered rather quickly, Ms. Rieger. Perhaps you'll feel differently once the baby comes.''

''We've been divorced six months, Mr. Pryor. There won't be any reconciliation.'' Not in a million years.

''Very well, then. Since the pregnancy was not recognized in the original divorce documents, we'll need to deal with custody and support.''

''I'm not sure I want Josh to know about the baby. I came here to find out what legal issues are involved.''

He leaned back in his chair with his hands behind his head. ''I don't see how you can keep it a secret. His name will have to appear on the birth certificate, and he'll be required to provide child support.''

A knot tightened in Ryanne's stomach. ''But I don't want anything from him. I can raise my baby myself.'' Maybe if she kept saying it, she'd believe it.

''I see.'' He leaned forward and twirled a silver pen between his fingers. ''So your personal finances are adequate to assume 100 percent of the child's support?''

Ryanne looked at the floor. Who was she kidding? She couldn't even support herself. ''No.''

Pryor put the pen to a yellow legal pad. ''What is your annual income, Ms. Rieger?''

The knot in her stomach became a lump and forced

its way into her throat. "I'm not working at the present." She wouldn't take pay for her time at the Perch, and gave her tips to Tammy who was saving for beauty college.

"But you will return to full-time employment after the baby's birth?"

She leaned forward. "Look, I'm not exactly on maternity leave. There is no job to go back to. I'll have to find something when the time comes."

"Do you have medical insurance?"

"No." She had Birdie. An old fiddle. Tattered dreams. Little else. "But I can pay you and the doctor."

Pryor smiled gently. "That's not my main concern. It seems to me that you need your ex-husband's help."

"No!" Ryanne realized her response was too adamant when she saw the look on his face. "It's just that I don't want any reminders of the past."

He glanced at her midsection. "Pardon me for saying so, but you'll always have a reminder."

"I know. But I haven't heard from Josh in months. I don't even know where he is."

"He can be located."

"He shouldn't have to pay for my mistake."

"Your mistake?"

"I should have been more careful. He never wanted a baby."

"If he knew, he might take responsibility for his child," Pryor said.

"Believe me, responsibility is not in Josh Bryan's vocabulary." Though kind enough, the lawyer made her feel like the irresponsible one.

The phone buzzed. He answered it, then covered the mouthpiece. "I'm sorry, I have to take this. Do you mind?'' He looked at the door, and she stepped through it, to wait in the reception area.

Her foot started tapping as soon as she sat down. Getting Josh out of the picture could be more complicated than she thought. She had hoped he could just sign on a dotted line and move on with his life.

What would she move on to? The lawyer's questions made her acknowledge the dismal reality of her prospects. When she'd first discussed coming home with Birdie, they'd agreed she should stay ''until she got on her feet.'' How long that would take depended on whether she pursued her music or took a conventional job. She wasn't ready to give up, but she had been in the business long enough to know the life of a struggling musician was not compatible with raising a child.

Stars could do it, of course. They had big motor coaches and nannies, people to sweat the small stuff for them. All she had was herself. How could she be a good mother if she was making the rounds in Nashville or living on the road, playing clubs and cowboy bars? She didn't want a pillar-to-post existence for her child.

And she would never leave the baby behind for someone else to raise.

She didn't have many options. She could quit performing and concentrate on writing. She'd been at it for years and had a portfolio of original songs and arrangements to peddle. Not only would writing be a creative outlet, it had real financial potential.

But there was a problem with that plan. Someone had to hear her songs. She and Josh had shopped her music around Nashville for months without luck. Either a publisher, or someone else influential enough to make things happen, had to hear it. She wasn't likely to meet any

connected people in Brushy Creek, and in the meantime
she needed to support herself and the baby.

With her limited work experience, her best chance
was staying at the Perch. Birdie would love it. She could
set up a playpen in the little office. Later, her daughter
could play in a back booth while she worked.

Talk about history repeating itself. It had been good
enough for her, but it was not what she wanted for her
child.

Gordon Pryor opened the door and motioned her back
into his office. "Sorry for the interruption. Where were
we?"

Lost in the land of slim and none? She sat on the edge
of the chair. "I don't want any loose ends. Isn't there a
way to terminate my ex-husband's parental rights?"

"Certainly." Pryor explained the legalities. "Once we
find him, papers can be served. If he signs, we can file."

Ryanne gave him Josh's last-known address and
Tom's hundred dollars, then told him how to reach her
when the papers were ready for her signature.

It was a plan, and plans were good, but dread had
come back to nibble on her confidence. She didn't expect Josh to get all righteous and demand to be a real
father. Yet, knowing him, she couldn't rule out the possibility of him finding a way to pull the rug out from
under her. He'd been jealous enough of what he'd perceived as her superior musical talent to do something
nasty just to complicate things.

If he did stoop that low, she'd fight him with everything she had. Hopefully, it wouldn't come to that, because she didn't exactly have unlimited resources. And
she didn't want to place an innocent baby in the cross-
fire.

Chapter Seven

Little Brushy Creek pulled out all the stops each summer to keep its annual Independence Day Festival on the map. Hundreds of visitors swarmed in from all over Oklahoma, Texas, Missouri and Arkansas, to celebrate the nation's birthday and spend their money. Such a significant source of revenue could not be left to chance, and weeks of careful planning went into making sure there would be, as advertised, something for everyone.

By 8:00 a.m. on the big day, the normally sleepy town was wide awake and braced for the onslaught of revelers. All six blocks of Main Street were closed to traffic. Men in bright-orange vests directed visitors to parking areas on the edge of town. Local businesses, including Birdie's Perch, closed their doors to give out-of-town vendors a shot at the paying customers.

Colorful booths filled with arts and crafts lined the streets. Concession stands added to the carnival atmosphere by offering Indian tacos, sugary funnel cakes and hot, buttered corn on the cob, along with hot dogs, barbecue sandwiches and cotton candy. Tempting aromas filled the air, enticing otherwise-health-conscious people to play Russian roulette with their cholesterol.

Red, white and blue banners snapped in the breeze. Patriotic bunting decorated the sides of the flatbed truck pressed into service as a makeshift stage. It was parked under a spreading oak in the city park, and young men crawled over it, setting up sound equipment for the day's live entertainment. A Tulsa radio station, broadcasting from a mobile unit, kept up a steady stream of disc jockey patter and music.

It was early, but people were already streaming in, lugging lawn chairs and picnic baskets, pushing strollers, and chasing excited youngsters. Everyone wanted a good spot to enjoy the parade and other festivities. Women spread quilts in the shade. Men gathered in small groups to discuss grain prices. Children romped in the grass.

In the chili cook-off tent, Ryanne watched Birdie add a few final pinches of spices to the huge pot of what she hoped would be prize-winning chili. The contestants had arrived early to set up camp stoves and mix his or her own blend of secret ingredients. The carefully supervised pots would simmer until the judging at four o'clock, after which the chili would be served.

Birdie, satisfied with her efforts, replaced the lid on the bubbling pot. "So where are you meeting Tom?"

"By the bandstand after the parade."

"I hear he's riding with the Roundup Club." Birdie wiped her hands on her apron.

"I think the rodeo queen twisted his arm," Ryanne said dryly. "Like dressing up in sequins and fringe won't attract enough attention, she needs a handsome rodeo champ riding by her side."

"You gotta watch out for them rodeo queens." Birdie was serious enough to make Ryanne laugh.

"I'll do that."

"It's going to be hot today," the older woman warned. "Don't get yourself overheated out there. It's not good for the baby."

"Yes'm."

"And be sure you drink plenty of water so you won't get dehydrated. That's bad for the baby."

"Yes'm."

"Oh, and you make Tom buy you some lunch. You have to keep your strength up. And remember, you're eating for two."

"Yes'm." Ryanne couldn't keep the mischief out of her voice. "And I'll look both ways before I cross the street, and I won't talk to strangers."

"Are you sassing me, young lady?"

"Oh, no, ma'am. I'd never do that." She grinned and gave the older woman a hug before turning to leave.

"Baby?"

"Yes, Auntie?"

"You have fun now."

"Yes, ma'am." Ryanne gave Birdie a smart little salute, spun on the balls of her feet and stepped out of the gloom of the tent into bright morning sunlight. The temperature was predicted to climb into the nineties, and she was glad she'd dressed for comfort in a red T-shirt and blue denim maternity shortalls. White leather sneakers ensured solid footing, and a jaunty red baseball cap, with ponytail streaming out the back, would keep the sun out of her eyes.

She strolled past the craft booths, admiring the items for sale. She stopped to try on a pair of dangly dreamcatcher earrings and was surprised when the proprietor of the booth called her name.

"Ryanne Rieger, as I live and breathe. I heard you were back in town."

Ryanne recognized her former classmate. "Kasey Pratt?"

The slender redhead leaned over the jewelry display to hug Ryanne. "It's Tench now." She wiggled her ring finger, displaying a gold wedding set.

"You married my old buddy Jimmy? When?"

"A year ago in June."

"I'm so happy for both of you."

"Jim's around someplace. I know he'll want to see you. How long will you be in town?"

Ryanne shrugged. "Things are kind of up in the air."

"Congratulations on the baby."

"Thanks."

"I heard about your husband," she said gravely. "I'm real sorry."

Ryanne stiffened at the look in her old friend's eyes. She never had been very good with pity. "Hey, he didn't fall down a mine shaft. He dumped me." Her tone said she was past having to whisper about it. "Let's get together sometime and catch up."

"I'd like that, Ryanne. My sister's taking over the booth at noon. I'll look for you later."

"Great. Oh, I almost forgot." She handed Kasey money for the earrings, but her friend waved it away.

"Call it a welcome home present."

Ryanne pushed the bills across the counter. "No, I can't let you do that."

Kasey slid the money back. "Just take the dang earrings. Can't an old friend give you a present?"

"Thanks." She tried to look grateful. She'd always

considered herself a giver, but lately all she did was take. Kasey was probably just being nice, but Ryanne felt as if the whole town had passed around her profit-and-loss statement. She understood small-town gossip. It would take another skunk infestation to relieve her of the burden of notoriety.

The parade started, and Ryanne stood with the children in front of the crowds lining the street. She watched the high school bands, the baton twirlers, the antique cars decked out with American flags and pretty girls.

A number of floats decorated by local Scout troops and 4-H'ers sported patriotic themes and ten-year-old Uncle Sams. Pet show entrants marched by, with everything from dogs and cats to ducks and pot-bellied pigs on leashes.

A group of Native American dancers stopped to perform to rousing applause, and Rotarians dressed as clowns passed out candy and balloons to the children. The mayor waved from the cab of a brand-new pickup, provided for the occasion by a dealership in Claremore.

The town's oldest citizen was Kasey's great-grandmother, one-hundred-year-old Ada Pratt. As a direct descendent of the founder of Brushy Creek, she was enthroned in a recliner in the back of another truck, shielded from the hot sun by umbrella-wielding children.

The foot marchers were followed by a couple of covered wagons pulled by mule teams. The Roundup Club brought up the rear. The riders were dressed in jeans, red shirts and black cowboy hats. The rodeo queen headed the group in a sparkly red blouse with chiffon sleeves, white jeans and a red hat with a feather in the band. As eye-catching as she was, Ryanne suspected most of the female spectators were too busy ogling the man riding beside her to notice.

Tom's boldly striped Western shirt, bolo tie and black hat were a blatantly masculine contrast to the young queen's rhinestone fluff. He grinned down at Ryanne as he passed on a prancing quarter horse. When he tipped his hat, she suspected she was the envy of every buckle bunny in the crowd.

Her heart turned over. It wasn't just he-man good looks, although Tom had definitely hit the jackpot in the gene lottery. She'd observed his interactions with others enough to know that even when he played strong and silent, he had a bulletproof credibility that made people trust him.

Tom Hunnicutt possessed an essential goodness that was obvious to everyone who met him. He wouldn't admit it, but he was a throwback to the chivalrous past. A man for whom scruples and principles were not just abstract ideas.

He was tough but kind. Hard but gentle. He would never twist a woman's arm in anger or use words to hurt her. He wouldn't blame others for his mistakes, as Josh blamed her for his lack of success. Tom had honor. A trait she was beginning to find very attractive.

After the parade Tom returned the borrowed horse, dodged the rodeo queen's come-hither looks and hurried to meet Ryanne at the bandstand. He stopped half a dozen times to say hello to folks who just wanted to tell him how sorry they were that he'd had to quit the rodeo.

Once, not long ago, he'd been sorry, too. Now he was glad those rough-and-tumble days were over. Like a man who'd finally beaten an addiction, he felt freer than he had in a long time.

He arrived at the bandstand and found Ryanne enrapt. She didn't just listen to the music, she devoured it. Her curly ponytail bounced as she tapped out the lively rhythm, and her eyes were filled with what could only be called longing. Caught up in the melody, she silently mouthed the lyrics to the song.

He'd never seen her onstage, so it was easy to forget she was a performer. What had she said? Something about performers needing to perform. Before she saw him, he slipped around behind the bandstand and motioned over the emcee.

A few minutes later Tom approached Ryanne as if he'd just spotted her for the first time. She smiled broadly and turned her attention back to the stage.

The next act was an ensemble of young clogdancers, the girls in frilly dresses, the boys in string ties and Western shirts. They tapped their little hearts out, and received rousing applause from the onlookers.

Ryanne grasped her big belly and grinned. "Hey, in ten years, my girl's going to blow them off the stage."

"Is she busy today?" Tom asked.

She nodded. "I've been having some cramps."

"That doesn't sound good."

"It's just false labor. I read about it in the brochure the doctor gave me. It means my time is getting close."

Tom leaned down and whispered in her ear. "If you need to lie down or put your feet up or anything, let me know."

Ryanne smiled at him. "Your concern is touching but misplaced. I plan to rock till I drop."

"Ladies and gentlemen." The emcee's voice boomed. "I have been informed that we have some homegrown talent in the audience today. Maybe with your help, we can prevail upon her to favor us with a song. Please give a big Independence Day welcome to Brushy Creek native, Ryanne Rieger."

The crowd broke into applause and Ryanne clapped right along with them until she realized it was her name that had been announced. She looked at Tom in confusion. He grinned and led her through the audience to the steps at the back of the bandstand.

"Are you responsible for this?" she asked under her breath as she smiled at the crowd.

"Who me?" Tom backed down the steps, shrugging off her question.

She barely had time to gather her wits before the emcee thrust the microphone in front of her. The crowd quieted with anticipation, and the band members shifted expectantly. She spotted Tom in the front row, and he gave her a big grin and thumbs-up.

From the looks of things, she would have to fiddle her way out of this one. Someone handed her an instrument, she tucked it under her chin and struck the opening chords of a lively Cajun zydeco tune. The other musicians jumped in, and before long the audience was clapping the beat.

By the time she got to the fiddle solo, Ryanne was bowing with such intensity she scarcely noticed that a hush had fallen over the crowd.

She couldn't see outside herself. She had surrendered her consciousness to the music, the notes whirling from her memory like a fountain of sound. The bow was alive in her hand, skipping across the strings with a life of its own, as her fingers found every chord with flawless precision.

The solo was complex, but she didn't falter. She'd climbed inside the music, and she knew every labyrinthine turn by heart. So that was how she played—from the heart.

Tom listened to Ryanne's music, and a feeling of awe

swept over him like a strong wind. He watched her expression change as the tempo escalated. With a start, he realized she wasn't just playing the fiddle. She'd become one with it.

He didn't know much about music or musicians, but he recognized beauty when he heard it. As her solo wound down and the other band members picked up the beat, her eyes lit up with mischief.

She winked at the delighted audience, then with a flourish of the bow, challenged the band to a "duel." Despite her advanced pregnancy, she skipped lightly around the stage, her animated face reflecting the fun she was having. The crowd didn't know how much they were being worked. By the time she drew out a final, resonating note, she had them eating out of her hand. They rewarded her with wild applause.

Ryanne returned the fiddle to its owner. Unable to bow to acknowledge the ovation, she plucked out the hem of her short overalls with one hand, placed the index finger of her other hand under her chin coquettishly, and dropped an exaggerated curtsy. This only elicited another burst of applause and calls for an encore.

The band gave their enthusiastic approval, as did the emcee. She turned and spoke to the musicians, then faced the audience again.

"Thank y'all for such a warm reception. It's great to be home again. I'm going to slow things down now with an old favorite." She took the microphone in hand as the guitarist strummed the opening chords of a Patsy Cline ballad.

"Crazy."

Yeah, that just about summed it up. Along with everyone else in the crowd, Tom was knocked on his can by the breathy alto wrapping around the torchy lyrics. He hadn't expected so much vocal range from a woman of her stature.

Admiration fueled misgivings. Ryanne was no amateur wannabe. Her talent eclipsed everything on the stage. He knew nothing about the music business, but he sensed the future as he listened to her pour herself into the song. Like an unseen planet in an unknown solar system, Ryanne was out there.

A star just waiting to be discovered.

His heart tightened. He'd been crazy, all right. Not only to build castles in the air, but to think someone like Ryanne might want to live in them. What made him think a log cabin on a hill would be enough for her? That he would be enough. He'd made that mistake with Mariclare. He'd lost her because he'd foolishly assumed his secondhand dreams were her dreams, too.

Ryanne had a future far from here. She would never get music out of her system. It was part of her. Maybe even the most important part. It fed her. It put a glow in her smile, a spark in her eye. How could he compete with that? She was blessed with a gift too big for Brushy Creek. No way could a place like this, or a man like him, ever hold her.

She wasn't finished with music. Not by a long shot. She was just gathering strength to tackle the world again.

The irony of the situation was not lost on him. Just when he'd started thinking about putting down roots, Ryanne was poised to spread her wings.

Ryanne belted out the final lyrics and left the stage to thunderous applause. God, it felt good. It had been so long since she'd performed for a live audience, she'd forgotten what a high it was. She loved the power she felt when she held an audience in her hand. The way her very existence was validated by the approval of strangers. Too bad she couldn't live her whole life behind the footlights. Onstage she was in control.

"I owe you one, cowboy," she told Tom when she found him in the audience.

"I thought you might need to exercise your vocal cords." He led her away from the crowd to a quieter area of the park.

"I really did need that," she told him. "Thanks for knowing." Was there anything about this man that wasn't completely charming?

"I didn't know," he admitted. "I guessed. I wanted to hear what you had to offer."

"And...?"

"You blew me away. I had no idea a little gal could make such a big noise."

"Is that right? So, what did you expect?"

He shrugged. "I don't know. A cross between Minnie Mouse and Betty Boop, maybe?"

She made a face. "And here I was thinking you were the last gallant man in the county."

They sat on the bench of an unoccupied picnic table and watched children playing on the swings. Tom was the first to speak.

"You're good, Ryanne. When you stepped onto that stage, you were transformed. It was some kind of magic. You should have made it in Nashville."

She sighed. "Thanks for the vote of confidence, cowboy, but there's magic on every corner there. Every salesgirl, every waitress, every secretary you meet is just waiting for a break. And they're all good."

"You've got so much going for you. The way you played that fiddle. God, you're talented."

She smiled. "You're sweet to say so. But in Nash-

ville, so is every cab driver and mechanic. I'm telling
you, you cannot spit in that town without hitting a musician. And they're all talented.''

"You're not afraid of a little competition, are you?''

Ryanne looked away, pretending to watch two small
girls play tag. Should she tell him about all the auditions? The ones where she'd been eliminated before she
ever sang or played a note.

Sorry. Too short. Too old. Too young. Sorry. Not sexy
enough. Not wholesome enough. She'd heard it all. She
didn't have "the look" they were looking for. Not country enough. Too country. She'd always seemed to be in
the wrong place at the wrong time.

Should she tell this good man how unkind people
could be? Admit that if she'd been willing to barter her
body for a break, she might not be here today? Could
she lay bare the years of humiliation and rejection that
had whittled down her spirit? Would he understand?

She studied his strong profile and decided to keep her
pain to herself. This was one time when there was nothing to be gained by sharing.

Chapter Eight

Ryanne was determined to put all serious thoughts aside, and have a good time. With the baby due in a couple of weeks, today was her last chance for unencumbered holiday fun. By Labor Day she would be toting infant paraphernalia and scheduling her life around naptime.

Tom's mood seemed forced, and he was even less chattier than usual. He smiled in all the right places, but it was not the smile of a man having fun. Ever since her performance on the bandstand, he'd seemed to want to say something he couldn't quite put into words. When she asked him what the problem was, he assured her nothing was wrong. She let it go at that, because the day was slipping away from her, and she loved the Fourth of July.

After chowing down at the watermelon feed, she cheered Tom to victory in the cow chip tossing contest. He bought her Sno-Kones and fed her funnel cakes to keep up her strength. When he complained about the come-on looks he got from other females, she said it served him right for spray painting his Wranglers on that morning.

Shortly before noon, they caught up with Junior and the widow Applegate. The elder Hunnicutt was trying to talk his lady friend into entering the hog calling contest.

"Come on, darlin'," Junior cajoled. "You know you could beat those other gals with one tonsil tied behind your back."

"Are you saying I have a big mouth, Junior Hunnicutt?" the red-haired widow demanded.

He looked at Tom and Ryanne, pleading with them to bail him out. "No, honey, it's not that. You've just got a powerful set of pipes, is all."

Ryanne waded in to save him. "Letha, I'll do it, if you will."

"Really?" The older woman seemed willing to be won over. "It would be nice to take that blue ribbon home. It'd give those gals over at Bingoland something new to talk about."

Tom's was the voice of reason. "Ryanne, you've never lived on a farm. Persimmon Hill may be in the country, but it doesn't count."

"So I'm not Old MacDonald." She shrugged dismissively. "How hard can it be?"

"Have you ever, in your whole life, called hogs?"

"Nope." The more he questioned her lack of skill, the more she wanted to show him she could do it.

"Have you ever even *seen* a hog that wasn't swimming in barbecue sauce?"

"Maybe not up close and personal. But I met plenty of two-legged pigs in Nashville. That should count for something."

"Come on, son," Junior interceded. "Give the little

lady a chance. She didn't interfere when you went for the cow-flop Frisbee ribbon, did she?''

Tom gave her shoulder a gentle nudge. ''Have at 'em, Miss Piggy.''

''Watch it, cowboy. That crack better refer to my vocal ability and not my shape.'' Ryanne hopped from foot to foot, throwing punches in an Rockyesque underdog dance.

She grabbed the older woman by the hand. ''Come on, Letha. Let's go call some hogs!''

Later, over a lunch of Indian tacos and tall cups of iced tea, Ryanne lamented their humiliating defeat. She threw an arm across Letha's shoulders and sighed. ''We were robbed, girlfriend.''

Letha frowned. ''I don't know. Tru Dildine grew up on a hog farm. Stands to reason she'd take the ribbon.''

''But she was so *predictable*.'' Ryanne dismissed the winner with a wave. ''Sooo-ee, sooo-ee, sooo-ee. What was that about? Doesn't creativity count for anything anymore?''

The men laughed at Ryanne's righteous indignation.

''Not with hogs it doesn't,'' Tom said.

''Hogs are creatures of habit,'' Junior explained with a chuckle. ''Don't feel bad, honey, they probably just didn't realize what you were doing up there was for their benefit.''

''But it was a classic vibrato rendition in coloratura fugato,'' Ryanne protested.

The others exchanged looks of bewilderment.

''Opera?'' She rolled her eyes at the obvious.

''Well, there you go,'' said Junior.

''Yep. That explains everything,'' said Letha.

''What?'' Ryanne looked around the table.

"Those hogs you were calling," Tom said with a straight face, "were country-western fans."

Tom and Ryanne left the older couple at the Ferris wheel. While looking over the arts and crafts booths, they ran into the Tenches. Ryanne was glad to see her old friend Jimmy and marveled at how happy he seemed. Teenage angst behind him, he and Kasey were obviously very much in love. They visited for a while, catching Ryanne up on the lives of old friends.

Everyone, it seemed, had settled down to adulthood with few audible shrieks of protest. Whether working in their daddies' businesses, teaching second-graders or operating their own Tupperware franchises, Ryanne's classmates had moved on.

Was she the only one who'd taken three giant steps backward?

"We heard you singing and playing this morning," gushed Kasey. "You are *so* good. Those people in Nashville must've been crazy to let you get away."

"Thanks." Kasey made it sound like she'd sneaked out of town under cover of darkness to avoid a lynch mob waving record deals and personal-appearance contracts. Too bad the people of Brushy Creek didn't run a record company. She'd have it made in the shade.

At four o'clock they made their way to the cook-off tent. They found Birdie dishing up paper cups of her Red-Hot-Mama Chili for judges who took their jobs seriously. They savored the spicy stew, then scribbled in their notebooks before moving on to the next entrant.

Birdie caught Ryanne's eye, and gave her a close-to-the-vest thumbs-up of triumph. It wasn't just confidence in her cooking skills that made the older woman cocky. It was the long tradition of blue ribbons decorating the walls of the Perch. Winning the chili cook-off was good for business.

No one was surprised when first place was announced, but Birdie had the good grace to look humble. Effusive in her thank-yous, she was savvy enough to throw in a plug for the café while she was at it.

She found Ryanne and Tom in the crowd and thrust two steaming cups of chili at them. "Eat up," she told Ryanne. "I know you must be starving."

Ryanne looked at Tom and then at the chili. She felt a little queasy. The excesses of the day were finally catching up with her.

"Actually, I'm not all that hungry."

"Come on," the older woman cajoled. "I really outdid myself this year."

"I'm sure it's delicious," Tom put in. "But Ryanne's had a few too many snacks today."

"Like what?" Birdie eyed her suspiciously. "You never eat enough."

Tom nudged her gently and Ryanne piped up. "I had a lot of watermelon."

"A heck of lot of watermelon. Didn't you have some cotton candy?" Tom prompted.

She nodded. "And a cherry Sno-Kone."

"Don't forget the grape one," he reminded her.

"And a couple of funnel cakes," Ryanne recalled.

"We had Indian tacos for lunch," Tom reminded her. "You ate yours and part of mine."

"Didn't I have an ear of corn?"

He winced. "Two, I believe."

Ryanne searched her memory. "Caramel corn. I had a whole bag of that."

"Are you trying to get out of eating my chili?" Birdie asked. "Or are you just aiming for a slow death?"

"I guess I got a little carried away," Ryanne admitted. "I wanted to sample everything."

"You always did have trouble with moderation, young lady." Birdie set the cups of chili on a nearby table. "When you want something, you just jump in after it. Don't ever stop to consider the consequences."

"I'm doing better," she protested. "I've been a model of restraint about some things." She sent Tom a sidelong glance, but he didn't seem to make the connection.

"Well, I hope you don't get sick. It wouldn't be good for the baby," Birdie said.

"I'll cut her off the junk food," Tom promised.

"Go on, then. Make way for people who can appreciate good chili. I'll catch up with you later."

They ducked out of the tent like scolded children and made their way back to the bandstand. When Tom draped his arm around her shoulders, his touch had an interesting effect on her. The skin under his hand started tingling, sending hot currents down her arm and into her fingers.

She wondered how it would feel to experience that warm, liquid sensation all over. If his palm on her shoulder could create an internal meltdown, and make her heart race with anticipation, could she survive whatever his lips might do?

She mentally smacked herself in the head. What was she doing? These were not the thoughts of a woman who'd recently declared a moratorium on men. These were the thoughts of a needy, clingy female who thought she couldn't get along without a man.

And that was exactly what she'd vowed *not* to be.

He removed his hand to applaud the performers and took the warmth with him. Lord, it had to be wrong for an out-to-there pregnant lady to have lascivious thoughts about a man who had befriended her. Window shopping was one thing, but trying things on for size was something else. She had to be careful. She couldn't afford to mess up again.

She needed a friend more than she needed a lover.

Birdie was right. She did rush headlong into things. She'd taken off for Nashville half-cocked. She'd leaped blindly into marriage with Josh. She'd impetuously set up limits with Tom.

She had to slow down and develop some caution.

At dusk Tom walked Ryanne toward the park to await the fireworks. They passed a young couple, giggling and holding hands. He smiled at the sleeping infant cuddled in a pack on the man's chest.

"You've been quiet all afternoon," Ryanne said as they neared the park.

"I guess I've been thinking."

"It's against city ordinance to think today. You're supposed to be having fun."

"I've done that, too."

She found a spot under a tree, commented that with her luck it was probably chigger town, and sat down in the grass. She sighed and said she hadn't realized how tired she was until now.

Tom dropped down beside her, one knee bent and the other long leg stretched out in the grass.

"I think it's about time," she said.

"Nah." He checked his watch. "They won't be starting the show for another half hour."

"I wasn't talking about fireworks."

"What then?"

"It's time for you to tell me about Mariclare. You've been thinking about her today, haven't you?"

Tom hesitated. "Among other things."

"So far this has been a pretty one-sided friendship, cowboy. I have problems. You fix them. I need help. You give it. I ante up with details of past indiscretions. You fold. I've told you mine. Now you have to tell me yours." The set of her jaw indicated that "no" was not an option.

He propped his hat on his knee and raked through his hair as he always did when he was thinking. He wanted to tell her. He needed to. He just couldn't get the words in order. He looked at her, and she smiled. She didn't try to hurry him. She just waited.

It was several moments before he spoke. "Remember me telling you how I lost my concentration in the chute that day with Hellbender?"

"Before your accident, yeah."

"What I didn't tell you was why I lost it. I think I want you to know about that."

Once they got started, the words rolled out of him like cattle from a stock truck. Bumping. Shoving. Anxious. Impatient to see the light of day.

"At the time, we were living in Ft. Worth. Mariclare had a nice apartment and was teaching art in a suburban high school. I stayed with her when I was in town, but I was on the road most of the time. There's a saying— If the rodeo don't kill you, the commute will."

"So she didn't travel with you?"

"No. She didn't go to many shows. She thought the rodeo was brutish. Violent. She didn't care for rodeo people, either. She wasn't a snob. She just didn't fit in."

"But she knew how important it was to you, right?" Her question urged him on.

He shrugged. "Sure. We grew up together. She knew rodeo was my thing. I knew art was hers. That was okay for a while, but the older we got, the more she was after me to quit. I was making good money by then. Hitting a hundred shows a year. Racking up points. I made it to the Finals every year. Won some world championships. Rodeo was my life.

"I told her I'd quit someday. We talked about returning to Brushy Creek and turning those eighty acres of mine into a quarter horse farm." He outlined his plans, from the log house on the knoll to the registered stock in the barns.

"And that's what she wanted?"

"I thought it was." He shook his head. "No. The truth is, I never asked her. I just *assumed* we wanted the same things." His smile was grim.

"What happened?"

"I was off rodeoing, planning for the future. She got impatient and went ahead with her life. Got a master's degree in fine art. Put some paintings in a gallery. Bought a dog."

"And?"

"And I knew something was up when she agreed to join me in Pecos. She hadn't been to a rodeo in over a year. She chose the day of my big event to issue her do-or-die ultimatum."

"Which was?"

"Quit. Or else." He hadn't wanted to believe she was serious. But she'd tagged after him right up to the chute, demanding he listen to her for once in his stubborn, hardheaded life.

"Just like that?"

"Right then and there. She said if I didn't walk away from that rodeo, that ride, she was walking away from me. She had an offer to teach art at some fancy private school in Connecticut. She wanted me to go with her."

"What did you say?"

"I asked her what the hell I was supposed to do in Connecticut." His jaw tightened. He recalled how he'd felt at being backed into an inescapable corner. Mariclare had wanted to force his hand and she'd succeeded.

"Surely you could have compromised."

"She didn't leave me much wiggle room. If I didn't go with her, she was going alone. She'd already accepted the job and had to report for work in two months."

"So she left while you were in the hospital?"

"I didn't give her a choice." And she didn't give him one.

"After you recovered and had to quit riding, didn't you try to work things out?"

Tom shook his head, a look of self-disgust on his face. He'd been too busy with his personal pity party to do much of anything.

"So that's what blew your concentration with Hellbender?"

"A back alley brawl with your fiancée in front of a crowd of cowboys can be a little distracting."

"She should have picked a better time. A better place."

"She tried. Lots of times. I wouldn't listen. I don't blame her." He was adamant about that. "I'm responsible for what happened."

He didn't harbor any hard feelings toward Mariclare. She'd been right. He *was* a self-centered SOB who put bronc riding ahead of everything else in his life. He *did* expect the world to spin on his timetable. And he never *had* considered that she might have wants separate from his.

He'd almost made the same mistake again.

Tom's clenched fists told Ryanne how much the confession had cost him. He was clearly a man in need of comforting. He'd been there for her when she needed it, and it was time to return the favor. After all, what were friends for?

Her first impulse was to hug him, but she placed her hand on his arm instead. "I'm sorry, Tom. You and Mariclare were together a long time. I know how much you loved her."

He'd picked a favorite tree and seemed content to stare at it. "Water under the bridge now."

His stubborn denial of his pain only made her want to hug him more. She wanted to take his head onto her lap and smooth his dark hair. She wanted to stroke his cheek where the dimple lived. She wanted to do whatever it took to make him feel better.

But she was afraid to touch him. Afraid of her own errant impulses. She had strong feelings for Tom, but they were feelings she didn't understand and couldn't indulge. She could not afford to be reckless again. She could never again think only of herself.

"Is it?" she asked.

"She's married. To a sculptor who's never even been to a rodeo. She's got her life now. She's happy."

"You deserve to be happy, too."

"I'm working on it."

Unwilling to look at Ryanne, Tom stared out over the little park. Families were eating picnic suppers, settling babies down for naps, catching their breaths. Now that the sun had set, the air would finally cool down.

"It's okay to let yourself love again, you know." She spoke softly, like someone gentling a frightened horse. "We all make mistakes. I got married too fast. You waited too long. I jumped on opportunity. You let it slip away. Life doesn't come with a money-back guarantee."

He looked at her and found her eyes glistening with unshed tears. The depth of her emotion, along with the strength of his response, hit him like a mule kick in the stomach. Dammit! Part of him wished they'd never met. He'd yearned after her from the first moment he'd seen her, barefoot and boiling mad at the bus stop.

Damn her for stopping by on her way to someplace else. Damn her for making his sad heart happy. He should hate her for reminding him he was still alive. But how could he do that when, God help him, he was falling in love with her?

He berated himself. Was it love? Or had he grown so weary of being numb that he'd jumped at the first chance to feel something more? For a year he'd kept the world away. He was crazy to let someone as elusive and free spirited as Ryanne break down his carefully constructed barriers.

Crazy.

He didn't plan what happened next. He didn't think about it or wish it or judge it. He just let it happen. He tugged her close and leaned his face into hers. Night had crept in while they weren't looking and wrapped a mantle of privacy around them. They could have easily been the only two people on earth.

Ryanne parted her lips and felt them tremble, tingle with the need to be kissed. She wanted Tom's touch and cursed the control that kept his mouth inches, miles, from her own. He looked into her eyes, and she wondered if he could see the need he aroused in her. Could he feel the heat from her body, as she felt the heat from his?

When had she started wanting him? When had touching him become so important? Today between the cotton candy and Sno-Kones? Or had it always been there, lurking, since he'd first stepped out of the shadows and into her life?

"We need to talk about this." Her moving lips brushed his. Talk was actually the last thing she wanted to do. Talking and thinking required checking in with reality. She preferred the fantasies that had sustained her since she'd met him. Her heart, her body wanted him to take her into his arms. Hold her. Make her feel cared-for and protected.

Her brain was pumping nonfunctioning brakes.

Then she saw the longing in his eyes. It was raw and exposed. Her heart burned with regret. Had she been shallow enough to think she could have fun, forget her problems for a while, flirt with this wounded man, and get off scot-free? He deserved better than that.

"Tom. Please."

He couldn't tell if she wanted him to stop or hurry up. The hell with it. He groaned and his lips slanted over hers. At first his touch was soft and tentative, but when her tongue slipped from her mouth into his, he lost what little control he possessed. It was the moment of impact when two souls collide. That was one of the last viable thoughts he had as he cradled the back of her head to increase the pressure between them. She was so sweet. Her lips were soft, giving. Hungry. She strained against him, and the fire was stoked.

But it was her little sigh of surrender that was his undoing. He groaned again. God, if a mere kiss could turn him inside out, what would happen when he made love to her? Would the earth move, as the songs promised? Or would he just melt into a big throbbing puddle of simmering testosterone?

And who the hell cared?

This was wrong, Ryanne thought. She felt the need

with which Tom caressed her. That same sense of urgency was in her blood now, sending out frantic hey-lady messages. Turning her insides to liquid. Playing havoc with her pounding heart.

Oh, how could this be wrong?

Before her mind collapsed and her body spontaneously combusted, the baby kicked her. Hard. Insistent. Asserting its undeniable presence between them. The fetus picks up where the conscience leaves off, she thought. It was pretty sad that, of the three of them, an unborn child showed the most sense.

"Dammit, cowboy!" Maybe she could hide her flushed and turned-on self behind righteous anger. "What the hell are you doing?"

He pulled away from her, his dark eyes amused. "If you have to ask, I must be more out of practice than I thought."

"You have no business kissing me." She was still shaking from the hit-and-run hormone attack.

"Maybe not. But you kissed me back." It was observation more than accusation.

"You tricked me." She wanted to jump indignantly to her feet, but she couldn't. Not without his help. How could she stalk off in a snit if she couldn't even stand up by herself?

He laughed. "How?"

"You opened up. You got too close. You were too cute. You actually *needed* kissing. That's not fair."

"What are you so mad about?" he asked calmly as he stood up.

She just looked up at him for long, bewildered moments. "Because this changes everything."

He gave a mock sigh of relief. "Whoo, thank goodness. There for a minute I was afraid it didn't make that much of an impression on you.''

"It's not funny. Now we can't be friends.'' She was almost crying. Her carefully constructed house of cards had been blown apart by the huff and puff of one beautiful, soul-stirring wolf kiss.

He folded his arms on his chest. "Okay. Explain that one to me.''

"We agreed to be friends. We had rules. Expectations. You crossed the line, cowboy.''

"So we reevaluate. You said we could do that.''

"Down the road. I was talking about way down the road. Someday. In the future. You have to reevaluate first. Then kiss. You can't kiss, then reevaluate. That's just wrong.''

"Says who?'' He shook his head as though clearing it of her buzzing words. "You act like we had a charter or something.''

"You've ruined everything.'' She slapped her thigh. "I am so disappointed.''

"Funny,'' he drawled. "You didn't act that disappointed while I was kissing you.''

She vented a long sigh of frustration. "Dammit! You were supposed to be the cautious one. The one who takes his time and believes in long engagements.''

"We all know where that got me.'' His words were as dry as an Oklahoma summer.

"But *I'm* the impulsive nutcase who doesn't consider consequences. I trusted you to be sensible.''

"I am sensible. Kissing you just then seemed like the most sensible thing to do.''

"Whatever. The problem is, I can't be your friend now.''

"Not a problem." He grinned. "I don't want you to be my friend. See, I've got these other ideas."

He reached down to pull her up, and into his arms. She scooted away. She was weak. Her judgment was impaired. She couldn't touch him. Not yet.

"There can't be anything else between us. I have things to do." She patted her belly as if reminding him of the most important thing on her to-do list. "I can't be jumping into some hot-to-trot relationship at this stage of the game."

His dark brows raised. "Hot-to-trot?"

"You think this is pretty damn funny, don't you?" She was losing steam. That was dangerous.

"I think you're being extremely hormonal. Think about it. There's nothing wrong with two people starting out as friends and ending up lovers."

She leveled a shaking finger at him. "We are *not* going to end up lovers. Never. Not in a million years."

"Never say never. It has a way of coming back to bite you in the—".

"There are two kinds of people in the world. Those you lean on and those who lean on you. I don't want to be a leaner for the rest of my life."

"You're not a leaner," he tried to assure her. "You've just been in a temporary jam."

"Look, I don't want a man in my life now. What I want, no, what I need, is a friend."

He grinned, and his overall level of amusement really ticked her off. "We can still be friends."

"No." She shook her head. "You don't get it. We cannot be friends now. We had an agreement, but that kiss was a deal-breaker. It just complicates things."

"How?"

"How? Now I'm going to have to avoid you, and that

won't be easy in a town this small. I'll try not to think about you, but I'll worry that I probably did screw up. *Yet* again. Thank you very much.''

The first of the fireworks displays exploded across the night sky like shattered stars. Each successive boom made the baby jump in utero, and Ryanne held her belly protectively. The sky rockets weren't nearly as spectacular as the internal fireworks launched by Tom's kiss.

Damn it! Why'd he have to go and do that?

She finally held out her hand so he could pull her to her feet. Looking up at him was a real pain in the neck. He held her hand until she took it away from him.

"Ryanne," he said softly. "Calm down. We can talk about this. It's not the end of the world. It just might be the beginning."

"No. Take me—ow!" An intense cramp tightened low in her abdomen. Was it a belly ache brought on by the orgy of eating she'd done today? Or the false labor the doctor had warned her about? Maybe it was a real, honest-to-john contraction. How could she tell?

You'll know, dear, you'll know. The doctor's words came back to taunt her. "I don't know anything."

"What's wrong?" Tom gripped her shoulders as if he could squeeze the correct response out of her.

"Ow! Find Birdie." She clutched her abdomen as another powerful wave of pain rolled over her. "I don't feel so good."

Chapter Nine

It didn't take Tom long to find Birdie, who assumed full military command of the situation. He tried to talk to Ryanne; there were so many things to say. But General Birdie said this wasn't the time, thanked him for his help and bustled Ryanne into the Jeep with the assurance that these things were best left to womenfolk.

Birdie felt they should drive straight to the hospital, but Ryanne suggested they wait as the doctor had instructed. When the pains stopped, as suddenly as they'd begun, they concluded it was false labor and went home.

Ryanne was relieved, yet disappointed. The false alarm was a wake-up call reminding her she would be a mother very soon. She was grateful for the reprieve but frustrated by the delay. She was ready to get the show on the road.

Back at Persimmon Hill, she couldn't relax despite Birdie's efforts to treat her like the queen of pregnant ladies. She'd been tucked in, plied with herbal tea, fussed over and fretted about. She lay in bed, trying to sort out her feelings.

She couldn't deny a strong attraction for Tom, but she had to be careful not to confuse simple attraction for that love thing. She'd done that before, with disastrous results. She also worried that what she felt for Tom was based on the need to find a ready father for her child.

Single motherhood was socially acceptable these days, but didn't females have an evolutionary imperative to ensure male protection of their offspring? *That* had been socially acceptable for thousands of years.

Later, when Tom called, she feigned sleep to avoid talking to him. She wasn't ready. She didn't know what to say. Or what to think. She couldn't get past that kiss. That heart-pounding, eye-opening, deal-breaking kiss.

"That was you-know-who on the phone." Birdie stood in the door, clearly not fooled by Ryanne's squinched-shut eyes. "He was a talking sack of nerves. What'd you do to that boy tonight, anyway?"

Ryanne attempted a bit of snoring to add drama, but Birdie didn't buy it. She winked one eye open. "You're not leaving until I answer, are you?"

"Nope. What happened between you two?"

Ryanne gave up the pretense and sat up in bed. "Nothing."

Everything.

Birdie fluffed her pillow and sat beside her. "Did he say something to hurt your feelings? 'Cause if he did—''

"He didn't hurt my feelings." He'd made her realize how powerful they were. Just as bad.

"Well, what happened, then?" Birdie was nothing if not persistent.

"Nothing." She squirmed under the older woman's sharp gaze. "Oh, all right. I know you're going to sit there and give me the evil eye until I spill everything. Have you ever considered working for the CIA?''

"Ryanne Elizabeth Rieger." When Birdie used her full name, it meant she'd reached the limit of the older woman's patience.

"He kissed me! There! Does that satisfy your need to know?'' She flopped back on the pillow and covered her eyes with her hands.

"Oh, is that all?'' Birdie got up and smoothed the coverlet.

She peeped out from behind one hand. "Is that all? Isn't that enough?''

"Barely adequate, I'd say.''

"What?'' Ryanne smacked the bed with both hands.

"You mean you didn't see it comin'?'' Birdie shook her head, looking as amused as Tom had earlier.

"No. We had an agreement.'' She detailed the terms of said agreement.

Birdie laughed. "That's what you get for making a deal with the devil.''

"This isn't funny. It's the end of our friendship. And I really need a friend right now.'' She used the corner of the sheet to wipe her eyes.

"I know. You're all mixed up.'' Birdie gave her a warm hug.

Yes, she was. This was the worst time in her life to make important decisions. Her hormones were running amok, and she needed to concentrate every ounce of her energy on her main priority. Which was to squeeze a seven-to eight-pound person out of her body and then somehow provide a decent life for that person.

"Wait until you've had the baby and things settle down,'' Birdie said. "Then you'll think differently.''

"No, I won't.''

"Sure you will."

"I promised myself. And my baby. I will not jump into a relationship with another man."

Birdie pooh-poohed that. "Shoot, honey. Tom Hunnicutt ain't just another man."

Ryanne's eyes narrowed. "Oh yeah? What is he then?"

"He's *the* man."

The certainty of her statement so blindsided Ryanne that she was rendered temporarily speechless.

Birdie took up the slack. "I can't believe you haven't figured it out. You're so good together. He's tall. You're short. He's serious. You're not. He's careful. You're reckless. He's got his feet on the ground, and you've got your head in the clouds. A perfect match."

"Perfect? Sounds like polar opposites to me."

"But you know what they say about opposites."

"Yeah. They attract. What you don't know is what happens next."

Birdie smiled. "You're just being a hardhead. Everybody knows you and Tom belong together."

"Everybody?" she wailed.

"The whole town's been talking about it. I think there's a pool to guess when the wedding will be."

"A what?" she screeched.

"A pool. You know, people make a bet, put in money—"

"I know *what* a pool is. I just can't believe there is one."

"I think Tub Carver started it."

"My God! This is beyond unbelievable. It's ridiculous. It's—"

"Just the way things are. Not much excitement in a town the size of Brushy Creek." Birdie patted her shoulder. "Now you get some real sleep. You have to be tuckered plumb out."

She shut the door behind her, leaving Ryanne alone with her emotions. "A pool," she muttered. The whole town expected her to *marry* Tom Hunnicutt. So kissing him must have been very gratifying to them all. Was she that predictable? The good folks of Brushy Creek had wagered her future over cups of coffee, under hair dryers. She was their primary source of entertainment.

Jeez, money had changed hands.

Apparently, the world would *never* run out of ways to humiliate her.

Then she had a worse thought. Tom knew. About the pool. The wagers. That's why he'd acted so smug tonight. Why he'd found the whole be-still-my-heart kiss and her subsequent hissy fit so damned amusing. He thought her vow to stand on her own, to avoid serious entanglements, was a joke.

Just like their agreement to be friends. He had never planned to honor that promise. And she'd played right into his hands. Naive little Ryanne. Didn't even know she'd been had.

Not hardly. She glanced at the bedside clock. It wasn't midnight yet. It was still officially Independence Day. What better way to celebrate freedom than to declare her own rebellion?

The sun would set soon, but the temperature was still ninety degrees plus, the humidity nearly as high. Heatstroke weather, but Tom had work to do. He drove the truck around to the barn situated on his acreage and started unloading the pipe he'd purchased for the new fence.

It had been three days since the big fireworks display.

That night at the park, Ryanne had exploded like one of the Catherine wheels shooting into the sky. Who would have thought one little kiss would set off such a blaze of emotion?

He'd tried to call her. To explain. To apologize. To do whatever it took. But she wouldn't talk to him. This morning, he'd driven out to Persimmon Hill where she had holed up like a bristled-up badger. She wouldn't even open the door. Had, in fact, yelled at him to go away.

Satisfied she had not collapsed in the throes of labor, he'd returned to town. At the Perch, Birdie had assured him Ryanne just needed time to think things out. He needed to think, too, and he went through two pieces of pie and three cups of coffee before he made up his mind.

He was not going to sit around and mope. He was going ahead as though Ryanne's little tantrum never happened. So what if she was talented? So what if she had a future in the music business? Even solid-gold singing sensations had to live somewhere. It might as well be with him.

He would build the ranch. And the log house on the knoll. He'd pour his heart and soul into making a home for Ryanne and the baby. She could spread her wings and circle the globe if she wanted to. But at least she'd have a place to come home to.

And if he couldn't change her mind by showing her how much he cared?

Well, dammit, he'd just get a dog.

That day at the bank the loan manager had listened with interest as he'd outlined what needed to be done. The old barn, which had come with the land, would have to be repaired before it would be sound enough for hay and grain storage. Stables had to be built. A training ring and track constructed. Wells and stock ponds dug. Then there was the question of fencing.

At the time the thought of all the post holes he'd have to dig to enclose the new pasture had damn near trashed his enthusiasm for the whole project.

Now he knew it was just what he needed. A project. A big patch of hot, exhausting work to keep his body busy and his mind off a certain little pregnant lady. If she needed time, he'd give it to her.

But he needed something to do.

"Need some help there, son?" Junior Hunnicutt pulled out a bandanna and wiped his face. Tom was working himself into a fizz, and the very sight made him sweat. "Nope."

The older man leaned against the truck and cleaned his nails with a pocket knife. "When you get that pipe unloaded, you want to cleanup and drive into town for supper?"

"Nope." Tom dismissed his father like a troublesome insect.

Unperturbed by Tom's terseness, Junior watched him heave ten-foot lengths of fencing out of the truck. "Want me to see if I can get up a poker game for later?"

"Nope." Tom threw out the last of the pipe and swung to the ground.

"Well then, since you're in such an all-fired chatty mood, do you want me to book us a spot on the latest talk show? Maybe they're doing 'concerned fathers and the sons who ignore them.'"

Tom removed his hat and wiped his forehead with the back of his hand. "Nope."

"Dadgummit! Are you going to talk to me or what?" Junior snapped his penknife shut.

Tom leveled a butt-out look at Junior. "Nope."

"So what's going on between you and Ryanne?" After much skirting of the issue, Junior finally got to the crux.

"That would be none of your business."

"Why are you acting like a horse's patoot, then?"

Tom looked up and grinned. "Genetic defect, I reckon." With that he ducked into the tool shed. Junior huffed along after him. "We need to talk."

Tom handed his father a post-hole digger and slipped his arm around the old man's shoulders. "You win, Pap. Help me dig a hundred holes, and we'll have us a regular father-son bonding session."

Junior thrust the digger back at Tom with a shudder of disgust. "Hell, I don't want to talk to you that bad."

Tom laughed and threw the tools into the back of the truck. He started the engine and leaned out of the cab to holler. "Hey, Pap!"

Junior walked back to his truck. He was late getting to Letha's. "Yeah, what do you want now, you smart-mouthed pup?"

"I love you, you ol' buttinsky."

Working shirtless, Tom rammed the post-hole digger into the ground and felt the intensity of the heat bore into his muscles. He'd set himself an exhausting task after putting in a busy afternoon at the store. But that's what he wanted. Something to wear him out, so he could fall asleep at night and not be bothered by the wrong kind of dreams.

By the time he found the bottom of the tenth hole, Tom realized the futility of his plan. The work was meant to keep his errant thoughts at bay. But in reality the purely physical nature of it actually encouraged his mind to wander.

Roman candles and skyrockets weren't the only
fireworks he'd experienced that night in the park. Kissing Ryanne had awakened needs he'd managed to ignore
for over a year. She'd started a domino fall that had
ended in serious thoughts of marriage and family.

He tossed the digger down and stomped back to the
truck for a drink of water. What he needed was a strong
shot of whisky. Too bad he'd quit drinking a few years
ago. The rodeo circuit had provided plenty of chances
to see what alcohol could do to a man, and he'd decided
that was one evil he could live without.

Like tobacco, which he was also craving. It was a
sorry state of affairs when a clean-living man was driven
to bad habits by a little snip of a pregnant girl.

He swigged from the cooler and let the water run
down his chin, his chest. Maybe a long, cold shower
would make him stop thinking about her. Damn! What
was so appealing about an egg-shaped woman who wad-
dled? She wasn't the only cute brunette with a sharp
sense of humor he'd ever met.

So how had this one breezed into his life and turned
everything upside down? She'd made him believe he
could do it all over again. Take risks, fall in love, have
a future. It was because of her that he was killing himself
in this heat. She made him want to make something out
of nothing. She made him want to prove to himself, and
to everyone in Brushy Creek, that he was the man they
thought he was.

She would also make him crazy, if he wasn't careful.

Unwilling to face the gamblers of Brushy Creek,
Ryanne hid out at home, finally giving in to the nesting
instincts that had plagued her for weeks. Submitting to
domestic frenzy seemed the best way to avoid thinking

about Tom, so she filled her days with sorting, dusting, cleaning, scrubbing, laundering and organizing. The likes of which the little house had never known.

"You clean like you're putting out fires," Birdie observed one morning as she watched Ryanne go at a twenty-year-old blueberry stain on the kitchen counter. "Be careful you don't hurt yourself with that scrub brush."

Ryanne stopped her zealotry in midswipe and glanced up like a woman possessed.

The older woman took a long sip of coffee. "I've seen preachers at save-your-soul camp meetings who weren't as feverish about driving out Satan as you are about getting rid of that spot."

Ryanne looked at the brush in her hand and burst into tears. "What's wrong with me, Auntie Birdie?"

Birdie crossed the room and gathered Ryanne into her arms. "Nothing's wrong with you, baby. What you're doing is perfectly normal."

Ryanne sniffled and left Birdie's embrace to sweep up a microscopic piece of lint that had the temerity to blow onto the just-scrubbed kitchen floor.

"So I'm not going crazy?" she asked as she straightened the salt and pepper shakers and wiped invisible crumbs.

"You're just feathering the nest. It's all part of nature's plan. You're just doing what any good mother does."

"Good." She plucked a yellowing leaf off the geranium on the windowsill and carried it to the trash can like so much toxic waste. Then snatched up Birdie's empty coffee cup and washed it furiously. "I was beginning to think I'd tipped over the edge."

Birdie chuckled. "You may be following nature's

plan, baby. But you're a smidgen more dedicated than necessary."

Ryanne smiled. Thank God for Birdie. Her wry wisdom had kept her grounded the past two weeks. Talking about Tom was off-limits. Even though Birdie sometimes "forgot" and reported on his visits to the Perch, she respected Ryanne's need for distance. She was intuitive, kind, competent and wise. She just wasn't the world's most conscientious housekeeper.

On one of her many search-and-destroy missions, Ryanne had found old magazines from the sixties stacked alongside yellowed newspapers from the same era. She'd had fun reading the articles, but felt no compunction about carrying them all to the trash barrels to burn. "I meant to get rid of those," Birdie had told her. "I just never got around to it."

Boxes of unused items found new homes in local church thrift shops. Rugs were taken out and not just beaten, but physically and verbally abused. Walls were scrubbed and painted. Upholstery was shampooed.

Closets, cupboards and cabinets were aired out, their resident moths, ants and mice unceremoniously evicted.

The kitchen appliances were demildewed and degreased. Fumes from pine cleaner and bleach watered unsuspecting eyes, and room freshener filled the house with the scent of country spice.

Outside, every contemptuous weed had been pulled, every blade of grass shorn. Ryanne had hired a high school boy to finally haul off the rusting washing machine, replace loose roof shingles, wash all the windows and paint the rest of the trim on the house.

Everything on the place that needed to be repaired, replaced, washed, pressed or fumigated, had been. The house was ready for the little dancer. The little mother was as ready as she would ever be.

One evening Ryanne waited outside for Birdie. She sat on the porch swing, whose chains no longer creaked, thanks to a shot from the trusty oilcan. It was nearly dark before the Jeep's headlamps bounced up the rutted drive. Spring peepers were in full voice down at the pond, and tiny bats swooped around the pole light, catching insects on the wing.

Birdie sighed as she eased down beside Ryanne. "Bad news today. My cousin Kibby died this morning."

"Oh, no." Ryanne took the older woman's hand in hers. "What happened?"

"She had a stroke while she was watering her tomatoes. Collapsed right there between the rows. Never knew what hit her."

Ryanne hugged Birdie. She hadn't seen Kibby Corntassle in years, but she remembered the dark-haired lady who'd made wild onions and scrambled eggs for supper the last time she'd visited.

"I'm so sorry, Auntie. I know you two were close."

"She sweetened my life. We were like sisters when we were girls. After I married Swimmer and moved up here, I didn't see her as much as I wanted to. I was meaning to go to Tahlequah to visit this summer. I just never got around to it."

"At least she didn't suffer," Ryanne said softly. "That's something to be thankful for."

"Kibby went the way she would have wanted. Quicklike. Outside in the sunshine, close to God. It was a good death."

They swung gently, their feet barely skimming the worn gray floorboards of the porch.

"When something like this happens, it makes you think," Birdie said after a while.

"About what?"

"Gettin' old."

"You're not old, Auntie Birdie," Ryanne assured her.

"Not yet. But I'm working on it."

"Will you go to the funeral?"

"I should have visited her while she was alive. Now I have to settle for a sorry goodbye."

The service would be held day after tomorrow. Birdie expressed concern about leaving Ryanne alone, knowing she would not wish to travel so close to her due date.

"Don't worry about me, Auntie. I still have a week to go and I haven't had any false labor for days. You need to be with your family. I'll be fine here."

"I'll leave tomorrow afternoon and be back Wednesday night. Don't you do anything foolish like having that baby without me," she admonished.

"I'd never do that," Ryanne promised, but the idea of being alone in the house, so close to term, did make her uneasy.

Birdie sensed her reservations. "I'll stay if you want me to."

"I want you to go, Auntie."

She patted Ryanne's hand. "You have been a good daughter to me. Even if our blood is not the same, our hearts have grown together."

"I can never thank you for all you've given me."

"No words are needed. You thank me by being here. By calling this place your home. By sharing your child with me. And by getting rid of those darn mice once and for all. I thought they would never leave."

Chapter Ten

Birdie left for the funeral in Tahlequah the next day. Feeling even blimpier than usual, Ryanne shuffled through the house, looking for something to do. Nothing. Thanks to her guerrilla cleaning tactics, there wasn't even an out-of-place magazine to straighten. She let Froggy in for company, but the old dog was no fun. He just curled up on the floor and went to sleep.

She baked a pan of brownies for supper and carried them into the living room. Reclining on the sofa, with the plate balanced on her belly, she leveled the remote control at the TV. An old movie flickered on, but even the saucy repartee of Tracy and Hepburn could not keep her mind off Tom.

She'd refused to talk to him, had even told him to go away when he'd stopped by to see her. Apparently, he'd taken her at her word. He hadn't called since. By avoiding him for two weeks, she'd stayed true to her vow not to get sucked into something she couldn't handle. She was proud of herself. She'd been firm. Resolute. Un-wavering.

Stupid.

She never expected to miss him this much.

She munched another brownie. Froggy gave her a look that could only be termed reproachful. Had Birdie secretly recruited the elderly canine as her stand-in food cop?

"What?" she asked around a mouthful. "It's comfort food, okay? It's supposed to make me feel better. I need it."

The dog just stared in his baleful, bloodshot way.

"I know I look like Jabba the Hutt, but this is a very chocolate situation. Go back to sleep, and let me suffer in peace." Her abdomen tightened with the familiar ache of the Braxton-Hicks contractions that had plagued her all day.

She reached for another brownie, but someone rapped on the door. Wishing for the assistance of a winch, she worked herself upright and lumbered across the small living room.

When she peeked out the window, her heart took a perilous leap. Tom stood on the porch in the waning sunlight, looking more gorgeous than a man had a right to look. He was dressed in worn jeans, a chambray shirt with sleeves rolled back on tanned forearms, and scuffed boots. He was hatless, his hair still damp from the shower.

Just seeing him there, all strong and capable, reassured her, and her troubled mind ceased its clamor. Tom was more comforting than double-fudge nut brownies any day.

She opened the door when she could no longer bear the separation. She didn't greet him or jump into his arms or demand an explanation for his unannounced arrival. She just stared at him through the screen, her insides jangling with pleasure.

He grinned. "Hi."

"Hi, yourself." She hadn't known how desperate she was for the sound of his voice. It worked better than chocolate when it came to making her feel good.

"Are you doing all right?" His gaze raked down to her bare feet, back to her face.

"I'm fine." Big as a house. Covered with crumbs. But otherwise fine.

"So, what have you been doing?" He sounded awkward. A man with something on his mind who was trying to get past the preliminaries.

"Gestating."

"Uh-huh." He shifted his weight uncomfortably.

"That's pretty much all I can do these days."

"I didn't think you could get any bigger, but I see I was wrong."

Enjoyable as it was, idle chat would get them nowhere. "What are you doing here, Tom? I told you I didn't want to talk to you." The baby suddenly kicked her, as if offended by the audacity of her lie.

"Can I come in?" He looked past her to the living room. "We're letting all the cool out."

She held the door and he stepped inside, commenting on how nice the house looked. Directing him to Birdie's chair, she offered him a cold drink and a brownie, then settled on the couch. As far away from his denim-clad maleness as the small room allowed.

He took a deep gulp of his iced tea. "I think you should know. I have an overnight bag in the truck."

"You're leaving?" She tried for calm, but the thought

of Tom driving off into the sunset made her feel anything but.

"Actually, I'm staying." He ducked as though expecting her to throw a nearby object at his head.

"What do you mean?"

"Birdie wasn't comfortable leaving you out here all alone. She asked me to keep you company while she was gone. In case something went wrong."

Ryanne knew it was true. It was such a Birdie thing to do. "Will that change the odds, do you think?" she asked crisply. "The two of us spending the night under the same roof?" At his confused look, she went on. "The matrimonial pool?" He looked even more confused. "Don't tell me you haven't heard about the bets?"

"Ryanne, what *are* you talking about?" He leaned forward, his hands dangling between his knees.

She fell back against the couch cushions and told him the whole story, from the town's collective interest in their love life to Tub Carver's wedding pool.

He laughed when he'd heard her out. "Is that why you hid out here?"

"I wasn't hiding," she denied. "I was cleaning."

"You refused to talk to me because you thought people were making a joke of us, and I was in on it?" He seemed insulted, as if she should have known better.

"Yes. But I had other reasons." Lots of them. Like not wanting to be affected by the way he said hi, for one. Not wanting to feel that warm, glowy sensation he gave her, for another. Or longing for something that could not be. Good reasons.

"This is the first I've heard about a pool."

"Really?" She hadn't wanted to believe he had duped her.

"I'd never lie to you." His dark eyes studied her. "You know that."

"Really?" She thought she might cry. Or laugh. Or both.

"I'm sure you were a rational person once. Before all this." He gestured at her midsection and gave her an understanding smile. "You probably will be again."

She sighed, and the truth poured out. "Oh, Tom. I'm so glad you're here."

"Really?" It was his turn to be skeptical. "Does that mean I can stay?"

"As long as you stay way over there."

Tom helped Ryanne eat the rest of the brownies, then insisted on making her a grilled cheese sandwich. It was at the high end of his culinary skills, but it had to be more nourishing than snack cake.

Working at the stove, he slipped back into the easy companionship of the past. He told her about his plans for the ranch. How he would start small. Buy some good breeding stock, train colts for the track. Build it up from there. Oklahoma was a good place for a quarter horse operation. Pari-mutuel betting was legal, and the state supported several pro racing tracks.

"So far, Hunnicutt Stables exists mainly in my head and scribbled on pieces of paper blowing around in my truck, but I'm beginning to think I can make it happen." He flipped the sandwich onto a plate and set it on the table.

"I know you can." She reached out and squeezed his arm.

His whole body ached to touch her. Before the air between them became too charged, before he lost his nerve, he excused himself and went outside. When he returned, he dropped a sports bag on the floor. Then, with a flourish, he unfurled a long roll of paper and spread it on the table.

"This is it." He felt proud as he pointed out various spots on the blueprint. "The barns, the track. The tack rooms. And this is the house. What do you think?"

"It looks wonderful."

But did she think it was wonderful enough to call home? That's the question he really wanted to ask. And he would. As soon as the opportunity presented itself.

"What's Junior think of it?" she asked as she finished her sandwich. "Will you continue working at the store?"

"You know Pap. He just wants me to be happy. He doesn't really need me anymore." Tom wondered if his father had put any money into the pool. He'd certainly encouraged Tom to spend time with Ryanne. "He's got someone else to help him now. He and Letha are getting married."

She grinned. "That's great. When?"

"As soon as they can get it together. She wants a church wedding with a reception and the whole works. They plan to ask Birdie to cater the food."

"She'll be thrilled."

"Some people might wonder if we're going to make it a double ceremony." He said it lightly, like a joke, but he was really trying to create an opportunity.

"Yeah, right." She pushed back her chair and placed the plate in the sink. As she walked ahead of him into the living room, he noticed her knuckling the small of her back.

"What's wrong?" he asked.

"Backache. The load is putting a lot of strain on my muscles. They hurt all the time these days."

He helped her onto a low ottoman and sat on a chair behind her. "Show me where it hurts. I'll rub it for you."

She hesitated. "I'm not sure that's a good idea."

But once he began massaging the ache, she stopped protesting.

She sighed and let her head drop back, her eyes closed. The slim, pale column of her neck was the sexiest thing he'd ever seen.

"God, that feels good," she said on a sigh.

Too good, he thought. His fingers worked across her shoulders, kneading out the stiffness. She relaxed under his gentle touch.

But he was far from relaxed. In fact, he didn't know if he'd ever felt more tense. It took all the self-control he possessed to keep from burying his hands in her hair. He needed to kiss her again. Slowly. Deeply. Completely. To experience that unbearable heat again and prove to himself that it was as incredible as he remembered.

Her limp body melted back against him, and his hands stopped their massage. He wrapped his arms around her shoulders, and buried his face in her sweet-smelling hair.

Peaches. She smelled like peaches.

"Ryanne," he whispered. "I love you."

Her silence told him he'd said too much. She wasn't ready to hear those words. She was scared.

No. She was snoring. The unmistakable sound of slumber escaped her lips, like a tired kitten's purr. He smiled. She had to be exhausted, poor thing. He gathered her into his arms and carried her to the couch.

He stayed there with her until the moon had risen in the night sky. Just sitting in the dark. Holding her. Loving her. Now that he'd made his decision, he was content to watch her sleep. He was grateful that fate had brought her into his lonely life. Finally he eased her down and covered her with an afghan. Then he settled in the recliner nearby.

He had a pleasant last thought before sleep claimed him.

Ryanne's lovely face would be the first thing he'd see in the morning.

She awoke at 1:00 a.m. when a tightening band of pain gripped her midsection. It didn't feel like another round of false labor. It was different. It started down low in front and spread in an ever-increasing wave to her back. It locked on there, squeezing like a powerful fist for several seconds before resolving into a lingering ache.

She sat up, disoriented for a moment in the moonlight that streamed through the windows. Then she saw Tom in the chair and remembered. She'd fallen asleep in his arms.

She watched the clock. At the eighteen-minute mark, another pain began. Slowly at first, but gathering power as it clawed its way across her abdomen and dug into her back.

Okay. The doctor had said a pattern would develop. She would not panic. She would wait. Eighteen more minutes went by, and the sequence began again. She placed both hands on her belly and felt it grow hard as the intensity of the pain increased.

When it was over, she sat up, alert and afraid. This was different. This was *it*. Just as the doctor had assured her, she knew with a mother's special sense that this was the real thing. The pain she'd just experienced was the rolling thunder of first-stage labor. It would only get stronger as her womb readied itself for the delivery.

The little dancer was on her way.

She levered herself off the couch and shook Tom's arm. "It's time."

"Time for what?" He woke up rubbing his eyes.

She smiled. "To go to the hospital." She went to her bedroom to pack clothes for herself and the baby. She turned around, and he stood in the doorway, as startled as a man who'd just found a live hand grenade in his pocket.

"You want to go get the truck started?" she suggested.

He raked his hand through his hair. "Yeah, right." He turned away and then came back. "You're sure?"

She nodded and closed her suitcase. Ow! Incoming. The doctor had advised her not to think of the life-bringing contractions as pains, but if this wasn't pain, she didn't know what was. "Tom? The truck?"

"The truck," he repeated on his way out the door, sounding for all the world as though he'd forgotten what it was.

"Hang in there, Ryanne. We'll be at the hospital soon." Tom flipped on the turn signal and pulled out to pass a slow-moving station wagon whose pathological observance of the speed limit had added several unnecessary minutes to their trip. The dark, winding road had prevented passing for several miles, but he could finally get up some speed.

"I'm fine." She hoped she sounded better than she felt. The maybe-if-she-didn't-call-them-pains-they-wouldn't-hurt-so-bad contractions were blitzkrieging at the rate of one every ten minutes now. While held in their grip, all she could do was focus and breathe through them. When they subsided she wanted to collapse and cry.

"Are you sure?" Tom's glance was worried. "You don't look fine."

"Actually, I'm trying to decide whether to pass out or puke," she snapped. "But other than that, I'm fine."

And not too cranky, Tom thought. The speedometer inched over the limit. He was banking there wouldn't be any law enforcement types lurking behind the bushes at this time of night.

Since leaving half an hour ago, his purpose in life had been to make it to the hospital in one piece and hand Ryanne over to someone who knew what to do. He sure as hell didn't.

He drove like a man possessed, every birthing scene from every TV show and movie he'd ever seen spinning through his memory like a newsreel. Boiling water. Scissors. Newspapers. Twine. Screaming.

I don't know nuthin' 'bout birthin' no babies, Miss Scarlet.

In fictional accounts of childbirth, there were always lots of moans of anguish. Sometimes the mothers even died. He stole a quick look at Ryanne. She wasn't moaning too much, and she looked very much alive.

"Just take it easy. I'll get you there in time," he promised. *Please, Lord, let me get her there in time.*

"I know you will." Ryanne slumped on the seat beside him and held her abdomen. She closed her eyes and tried to stay calm for Tom's sake. The unflappable cowboy was close to freaking out and *that* made her nervous.

"Just try to relax. Breathe or something." He reached over and tuned the radio to a country music station, hoping to distract her. "It won't be long now."

"That's what I'm afraid of," she muttered. "Ow!"

Tom passed worry and went directly to panic. "Are they getting closer together?" *Please. Don't let them get closer. Not yet. Not now.* He drove with one eye on the road and the other on Ryanne who was breathing noisily through another contraction. The Dixie Chicks provided background music.

"Eight minutes apart. You know, this is so much harder than I thought it would be. I'm trying to remember what I read in the pamphlet, but I think my brain may be shutting down from lack of involvement. All I can think about is what's happening in my belly."

"This is just the first stage, though, right?" He needed reassurance. "You have a long way to go before the baby comes. Right?" *Please tell me you have a long way to go.*

"Right. This part could last a while."

"That's good." It was supposed to be Birdie, the rock, in the driver's seat, he thought. Not Tom, the chicken liver.

"Yeah, I'd hate for the fun to end." Ryanne shifted on the seat, but couldn't seem to get comfortable.

"I didn't mean it like that."

"I know." Ryanne took a deep breath and tried to relax as another wave of don't-call-it-pain rolled over her. She visualized herself riding the crest of the contraction, just surfing the wave, as she breathed in and out. Deeply, calmly. She could do it. If she stayed focused.

She wanted to participate fully in a completely natural birth. She didn't want medications or mind-numbing drugs. To do it her way, she had to take control. And hang on to it for dear life.

"Have I thanked you yet?" She sounded as if she'd just run a mile in high heels.

"Yeah, sure. You're welcome. No problem." Why was *he* short of breath?

"I didn't mean to drag you into this. What lousy timing, with Birdie gone and all."

"Really, I'm happy to help. Not that I've been much actual help so far."

The Claremore city limits sign flashed by. They were only minutes from their destination. She began to think they really *would* make it in time.

Another song came on the radio. After a few beats, she exploded in spluttering curses. "Why, that low-life, back-stabbing, brain-dead weasel!"

Her vitriol in the midst of everything else, took Tom completely by surprise. "Who are you talking about?"

"Shush!" She signaled for quiet and punched up the volume on the radio. Popular singer Matt Clancy crooned about being branded by some woman's love. "That's my song!" Ryanne smacked the seat. "He stole my song! I can't believe it!"

"Matt Clancy?"

"No, no, no. Not him. Josh. It had to be Josh. He sold my song to Matt Clancy."

At the end of the piece, the deejay announced "Branded" as Clancy's new single, and predicted it would be a hit.

Fuming, Ryanne reached over and flipped off the radio, and pounded the dash. "That double-crossing son of a—"

"Would you care to explain what's going on?"

"I wrote 'Branded.' My God, he didn't even change a word of the lyrics or a chord of the music. He finally got a cut with my song. Damn him!"

"You think your ex-husband sold your work?"

She gave him a look. "I *know* he did. And he passed it off as his own. There's no other way Clancy could have gotten it. What am I going to do?"

"For starters, you're going to have a baby. You'll have to sort this other stuff out later."

"I am so mad! I want to whack him upside his wooden head! No. I want to kill him! Ow!" She gripped her belly.

"Look." He looked relieved when the well-lit hospital complex loomed into view. "We made it."

Thoughts of music, mayhem and everything else were forgotten as Ryanne breathed through another contraction. Tom pulled around to the emergency entrance and parked. As he helped her out of the truck, a gush of warm liquid ran down her legs.

"My water just broke." She felt a sense of wonder.

"My God! What do we do now? Can you walk? Should I carry you?" Tom picked up her bag and set it down again. Picked it up. Put it down.

"It's really going to happen," she whispered. "I'm having a baby."

"Was there ever any doubt?"

Ryanne smiled. "I still can't believe it. I'll walk into the hospital as one person. But when I walk out, I'll be forever tied to another human being. My life will never be the same. There will always be someone whose happiness is more important to me than my own. It's an incredible feeling. Knowing everything is about to change. Forever."

Tom was staggered by the radiance of Ryanne's expression. She was so beautiful, and he loved her so much. Still, it did not seem like the time to stand around rhapsodizing about the joys of parenthood. He picked up the bag and nudged her.

"If it's all the same to you," he said. "I'd rather you had the baby inside under a doctor's supervision. Not out here in the parking lot."

The next few minutes were a blur as a nurse whisked Ryanne away, leaving Tom to deal with the detail-oriented admitting clerk. He was in the middle of explaining, for the third time, that it would be a cash transaction, so there would be no insurance forms to file, when the nurse came back and grabbed his arm.

"Sorry, Papa, but you need to come with me. Mama's at eight centimeters, and things are moving fast."

"But I'm not—"

"We'll be lucky if Dr. Scott gets here in time." She ushered him down the hall.

"But I'm not—"

"Don't worry now, Mama's doing fine, but she needs you to help her through this."

"But I'm not—"

"Oh, yes, you are. Little mama needs you, so change into these and get in there." The nurse thrust a set of green surgical scrubs into his arms, then disappeared through a door marked Labor and Delivery.

A few minutes later he cautiously pushed open the same door and was immediately accosted by the no-nonsense nurse whose name tag identified her as Carole P.

"Well, there you are, Papa. I thought we were going to have this party without you." She grabbed his arm and steered him into the room where Ryanne was sitting up in a big bed, hooked up to some kind of monitor. She wore a faded hospital gown and had an IV drip taped to the back of her hand. Her hair was damp with sweat, and she was huffing and puffing to some internal rhythm. Her eyes widened when she saw him, but she didn't miss a puff.

"Get over there." Carole P. seemed to sense his hesitation. "She didn't get herself into this alone, and she shouldn't have to get herself out of it alone, either."

Tom considered grabbing the nurse's shoulders to explain that he was not the father of Ryanne's baby and could not be held responsible for anything that was about to happen.

Then he looked at Ryanne. She was so small, so scared. She was working hard, held fast in the grip of something powerful and wonderful and terrifying. He kept his mouth shut. Maybe he wasn't responsible for her condition, but she did need him. He was all she had at the moment.

He turned to Carole P. "Tell me what to do."

The nurse grinned. "That's the spirit."

"Hi." He took Ryanne's hand in his. "Everyone seems to think I'm—"

"I know. I let them think that so you could stay. I don't want to go through this alone. I'm afraid."

"You may be afraid, but I'm scared spitless." He wasn't sure he'd be much help.

Her grin was a weak imitation of the real thing. "Your part is easy. I drew the short straw. Please stay."

He squeezed her hand. "We're going to do fine."

The nurse taught him how to time the contractions and focus Ryanne's breathing. Because she had painful back labor, he learned to massage the tension. He spooned ice chips into her mouth and wiped her face with a cool cloth. He murmured words of encouragement, held her hand.

Dr. Scott arrived, completed his examination, and proclaimed everything in good order, keep up the good work.

As dawn thrust the first tendrils of gray light into the room, the doctor announced Ryanne almost fully dilated. He praised her stamina and offered her a final opportunity to receive the epidural that would block the pain of the coming birth.

"I've made it this far," she said. "I think I can get by without it."

"You're the boss." Dr. Scott checked the fetal monitor. "Everything's fine. I see no reason not to do it your way."

"I want the whole experience," she explained, first to the medical team, then to Tom.

Dr. Scott laughed and patted her arm. "We'll see how you feel about that after you've *had* the whole experience." He and the nurse left with a promise to be back soon.

Ryanne relaxed against the pillows between contractions.

Tom had learned to read the monitor and recognized another one rolling in.

She gripped his hand, indicating he should start timing. She was panting heavily by the time it was over.

He was also out of breath. "That one was powerful."

She smiled. "Oh, you noticed."

They gave up trying to talk. The contractions came hard and fast, one after another, giving little time to regroup. It was the beginning of the next stage of labor.

Her eyes were wide, and she was short of breath. "Get Dr. Scott in here. I need to push."

The doctor came in and examined her. "You're not quite ready."

"That's what you say," she grunted. "I—want—to—get—this—kid—out! Now!"

"No, Ryanne." The doctor was kind but firm. "Not yet. Get ready for another contraction, and breathe through it."

"Don't tense up. Relax. Don't push, Ryanne. Breathe."

"Dammit! I don't want to breathe! I want to push!" She reached out and whacked Tom on the arm. "Help me. Tell him I have to push!"

"I think you should listen to the doctor." He didn't know what else to say. Ryanne's eyes were as wide and wild as a panicked mare. He hadn't known laboring women went a little crazy when delivery was imminent.

"You're both idiots!" she cried. "You're men and you're idiots! You don't know anything about it!" She was in tears. "Nurse, tell these, men, to let me push."

"Doctor's right, dear," Carole P. soothed. "Just a few more contractions."

Ryanne rolled her head on the pillow. Her control seemed to be slipping away and that terrified her. She squeezed Tom's hand.

He looked up for help, but the doctor was busy at the other end of the bed.

"Okay, Ryanne." Dr. Scott was ready. "I want you to push on the next contraction."

She gave him a murderous look. "Don't worry, I will." She grunted and pushed. Sweat beaded on her face and dampened her hair. Her lips were dry. Her skin streaked and blotchy with the strain of bringing a new life into the world.

To Tom she had never looked more beautiful.

Ryanne had only a moment's respite before beginning the process all over again.

And again and again and again.

Tom couldn't take much more. He was exhausted. His back hurt. His arms hurt. Even his feet hurt. His mouth was dry. He had a headache. Thank God he had the easy part.

"You're almost there." The doctor encouraged from the end of the bed. "We need a big push on this next contraction."

She fell back, limp and worn out. "I can't."

"Yes, you can." All three of them answered as one.

"I thought I could do it, but I can't."

"Get ready," warned the doctor. "Here it comes."

"No!" She began crying. "I'm too tired. I don't have the strength."

Tom leaned over and stroked her face. He spoke softly. "You can do it, Ryanne. You want to see your baby, don't you? Come on now, honey."

"Please, Tom," she pleaded. "Make it stop. I can't."

"Give it your best shot."

She opened her eyes and stared at him. He'd seen that look in the eyes of damaged horses waiting for the mercy of a bullet to end their pain. "Please, Tom."

He held her hand, flooded by powerful feelings. He loved this woman. He would be strong for her. "Listen to me. When the doctor tells you, I want you to push."

"I can't," she said weakly.

"But I know you can." He'd come into this with no idea how long and hard it would be. Now that he knew, he was humbled by the enormity of what he was asking her to do. She would have to transcend all limits. God, he loved her. He kissed her gently on the forehead.

"Get ready, honey. Show 'em what you're made of."

Ryanne was tired to the bone. She'd been at this for hours. Days. Her whole life. She couldn't remember a time when she wasn't pushing. She had no past. No future. There was only this moment, this pain, this monumental torment that engulfed her and devoured her from within.

She'd been a fool to think she could do this. She needed chemical assistance, but it was too late for that. Nothing could help her. No one could save her. She felt another contraction. Pulling, twisting. Ripping its way through her body like a May tornado.

She opened her mouth to tell Tom she was sorry. She couldn't do as he'd asked. She was giving up, and damn the consequences. She didn't have a push left in her.

But somehow she did. At the height of the contraction, an amazing thing happened. She no longer heard the doctor's instructions, or the nurse's encouragement, or Tom's fervent, whispered pleas. She heard her baby. Her daughter. A little voice that told her to be strong because it was almost over. A few more pushes and they could begin their life together.

She listened to that inner voice. She closed her eyes and pushed.

Suddenly the voice was outside her. It was the lustiest, most beautiful sound she'd ever heard. She squeezed Tom's hand and saw tears running freely down his cheeks.

She had no tears for this moment. She was too happy.

"And we have a baby!" the doctor exclaimed as he held up the dark-haired angel for them to see. "It's a great big beautiful girl!"

Chapter Eleven

Ryanne awoke from a dreamless sleep. The shades were closed against the afternoon sun, but insistent rays peeked through the slats and bathed the room in muted light. Tom sat in the rocking chair across the room, a pink-wrapped bundle snuggled in his arms.

She watched as the big man rocked gently, humming a tuneless lullaby. The baby's tiny fist escaped the blanket to curl tightly around one tanned finger. With his other hand he secured the knit cap on the downy little head. They had no blood connection, but she knew the tender newborn and the tough cowboy would always share a bond.

She was filled with a love so overwhelming and confusing it threatened reason. Her infatuation with her new daughter was easy to understand. But her mixed-up feelings for the man who'd helped bring her into the world were far more complicated.

Last night she'd only pretended to be asleep when Tom whispered his declaration of love in her ear. The whole time he'd held her, safe and secure within his arms, she'd fought the tears that would have betrayed her.

She'd known before he said the words. Earlier, when he showed her the plans. A single man didn't need four bedrooms. He wasn't building a house for himself. He was creating a home for a family.

The joy she felt for her newborn daughter was tempered by a deep sadness. As much as she cared for Tom, she could not take what he was determined to offer.

Tom lost track of time. He was fascinated by the way the baby's tiny, petal-soft features wrinkled in her sleep, the way her rosy lips pouted and puckered as she responded to internal cues. She'd only been in the world six hours, yet she had already wiggled her way into his heart.

He marveled at her size. She seemed far too small to be real. How was it possible for a whole human being to fit in such a tiny package? She squeaked and squirmed, but did not wake. Filled with protective instincts, he wanted to believe she slept so soundly because she felt safe in his arms.

"How long have I been asleep?" Ryanne sat up in bed.

"A couple of hours." He carried the baby to her. "Ready for a little visitor?"

She smiled, and held out her arms to receive the sweet-smelling bundle. "How long have you had her?"

"Nearly an hour." His arms felt empty without the baby's slight weight. When the nurse came in and found Ryanne out of it, she'd automatically deposited the child in his lap. He'd almost protested. Now he was glad he hadn't. He would always cherish the quiet time they'd spent together.

Ryanne stroked the baby's cheek with her fingertip. "She's beautiful, isn't she?"

Tom smiled at the little pink face. "Looks just like you. Oh, I finally reached Birdie. She was beside herself when I told her you'd rushed the job."

"She'll get over it."

"The funeral's at two. She said she'd leave as soon as she could and come straight here."

Ryanne laid her child on the bed beside her and opened the blanket swaddling. She stroked the little arms and legs, so pink and perfect. She touched the barely-there toes. The transparent fingernails with the tiny half-moons.

"I can't believe she's here." Ryanne gathered her up and lifted her gently to her shoulder, touching her lips to the dark, down-covered head.

"What are you going to call her?" He was already crazy in love with the little girl. It was time she had a name.

"What do you think of Hannah Rose?"

He repeated the name. It rolled easily off his tongue. "I like it. It suits her."

"It's strong," she said. "I think she'll do it justice."

Tom had no doubts about that. Ryanne didn't realize how resilient and self-sufficient she really was. She would raise her daughter to be the same. She would be a good mother. "Thank you for letting me be part of Hannah's birth day."

She smiled. "I couldn't have done it without you."

"Sure you could have," he scoffed. "You drew the short straw, remember?" His love for her had grown during the long labor. He'd watched helplessly as she'd stubbornly pushed her small body to the limit of her endurance, refusing the medication that would have eased the way. He'd wanted to shield her from the pain. Make it his own. But it was hers alone, and she had acquitted herself beautifully.

He knew now there were no limits to what she could do.

"I wouldn't have wanted to," she insisted. "I want you to know how much our friendship means to me."

"Ryanne—"

"I overreacted that night at the fireworks. I shouldn't have gotten so upset. It was just a kiss. I know it didn't mean anything."

"You're wrong," he said. "It meant everything to me." It was now or never. There wouldn't be a better opportunity. He held her hand and wished he had more to offer. But all he had was himself. "I love you, Ryanne. I want to spend the rest of my life with you."

"Tom—"

"Marry me. You can work on your music. Write. Perform. I'll support whatever you want to do. The ranch can wait until you get your break. I can work in the store. Drive you to auditions. Whatever you want."

"Tom, listen to me."

He couldn't listen. He had to say it. All of it. "I want to help raise Hannah. Be her daddy, and watch her grow up. I want to be there for you. For both of you."

"Tom, please."

"We found each other for a reason. I know you think it's too soon, but I don't want to wait. I'm done with waiting. I want you in my life." Funny, he would've thought laying his heart on the table would be harder than this. But now that he had no doubts to hold him back, the words came easily. They felt natural. Right.

Tom's earnest proposal touched Ryanne's heart, and indecision cut it like a knife. His offer was tempting. She was tired of battling the dragons of everyday life. It would be easy to slip permanently into damsel-in-distress mode and let Tom be her knight in shining armor forever. She'd thought she'd finally hit bottom that night at the bus stop. But Tom had been there to rescue her. And he'd been rescuing her ever since. In fact, their whole relationship was based on that very dynamic.

Maybe what he thought was love was only his misguided desire to continue protecting her. And Hannah. She'd seen the way he looked at her daughter. Of course he would want to protect a small, helpless child. He wanted to be there for them, as he hadn't been for Mariclare. It was a noble gesture, but she did not want his caring for them to be the way Tom Hunnicutt proved something to himself.

He was a good man, and she cared deeply for him. It would be simple to let herself depend on his steady love and support. To place her problems in his capable hands. The whole town had made wagers on just when she'd take the easy way out. When she would marry the man who offered her and her baby, not just a home, but a life. The life she'd dreamed of.

It would be easy. But it would be wrong.

"I'm sorry, Tom," she said softly. "I can't marry you."

His wide, hopeful smile dissolved slowly, as if he had not considered the possibility of rejection. "Why not?"

"Because I would never know if I married you for love or security. It wouldn't be fair to you. You deserve someone with no ifs, ands or maybes attached."

"Don't make a decision now," he said. "Think about

it. We can discuss it in a few days, once you get home—''

''No. I won't change my mind.'' She looked into his eyes, and they were dark with pain. She'd hurt him. God, she hadn't wanted to do that. But she had to be firm. If she wasn't, she might crumble and take what he offered.

And then she would never know.

She held Hannah close. She was a mother now. She had to be strong for her child. Make a life for herself. Stand on her own.

Stop leaning.

''But we've shared so much,'' he protested. ''I thought it meant something to you.''

''It does. But I think we've shared too much. Don't you see? We haven't had a courtship. We haven't even dated. We don't really know each other. I've just been poor, pregnant little Ryanne, always needing help. And you've been big, strong Tom, always needing to give it. A relationship formed during a crisis doesn't last. Not once things get back to normal. And we don't even know what normal is for us.''

''A crisis. You think we're a disaster, is that it?'' He sounded tired, like he was grappling with the inevitable.

''No. We're friends. Marrying for the wrong reasons—that would be a disaster.''

''I'll give you a courtship. We'll start fresh. Right now.''

''No.'' She would be firm. She would not be tempted. Her fingers tightened in the baby's blanket, to keep from reaching out to him. ''I need time, Tom. I'm not ready.''

He was quiet for long moments. ''Well, okay, then.'' He stood and started for the door. ''I guess there's nothing left to say.''

''Tom!'' She couldn't keep the plea out of her voice.

She wanted him to understand. Not walk away. She had to know he would be a part of her life. She couldn't lose him. "We can still be friends, can't we?" Please.

He turned around, his face tight with resignation. "I don't think so, Ryanne. I don't want to be just your friend. I think you've known that all along. I love you. I've always loved you."

She wanted to tell him she loved him, too. But that would only complicate an already complicated situation. "Tom, I never meant to hurt you, but—"

"No buts, Ryanne. I want to be your husband. Your lover. I want to be Hannah's daddy. Being your friend would be like feeding a starving man air. It just wouldn't be enough."

His expression changed, as though he'd suddenly solved a weighty problem. He strode back to her bedside, took her face between his hands and kissed her. A deep, fulfilling kiss that stirred her blood with unspoken promises.

Then he kissed Hannah's cheek. "I'm going to change your mind, Ryanne."

She could only stare at him, her lips still tingling from the heat.

"I heard from that stock contractor I did some work for. He wants me to check out a couple of horses for him in Nevada. So I'm going. But I'll be back. While I'm gone, I want you to think about me. About this."

He held her face and kissed her again. His tongue probed the recesses of her mouth, daring her to return it.

She did. With reckless abandon.

He let her go, and she fell back on the pillow, her heart pounding at a dangerous tempo. She touched her lips, hoping to hold on to his warmth as long as she could.

"Think about me, Ryanne," he said with a smile.

She started missing him before he even walked out the door. How could she think of anything else?

According to Birdie Ryanne was a natural-born mama. She discovered that mothering was the most rewarding thing she'd ever done. After a while she knew she'd escaped Rose Rieger's legacy of inadequate parenting.

She had never expected to feel so competent, nor had she imagined loving anyone as fiercely as she loved Hannah, who rewarded her mother's devotion by behaving like the earthbound angel she resembled. Birdie proclaimed her a "good" baby. But in the estimation of everyone whose heart she stole at first sight, Hannah Rose Rieger was a perfectly delightful, pinkly pretty, gem of a child.

She slept soundly in the beautiful antique cradle with the gossamer canopy. It had been waiting at Birdie's when they returned from the hospital. Tom had written no message other than "Sweet Dreams" on the card. Tucking her sleeping daughter beneath the downy comforter, Ryanne recalled the day she'd admired the cradle in the antique store window.

Tom had assured her she would make her baby feel loved, even if it had to sleep in a dresser drawer. That he'd gone back on his own, and purchased it to surprise her, only made her cherish the memory more.

Every time she thought of him, which was every single day, she hoped she hadn't made a major mistake by refusing his proposal. She didn't want to build her new life over a shaky foundation of regret, but the doubt was there, gnawing at her resolve.

The longer he was gone, the more she wanted an end to the separation. She was hungry for word of Tom, but the Brushy Creek grapevine was temporarily out of order. Gossip was suddenly missing in a town that thrived on it. Not knowing where he was or what he was doing only made her think about him more. As perhaps it was meant to do. She began to suspect a town-wide conspiracy to keep her guessing, and test the theory that absence did indeed make the heart grow fonder.

She tried worming information out of Junior, but not even blackberry cobbler would loosen his tongue. He ate the pie, then admitted only that Tom was his best man and would be home for the wedding at the end of August.

Birdie had agreed to cater the reception, and Letha spent many hours with her in the Perch planning the menu. Ryanne hung around, offering advice in between efforts to weasel news of Tom out of them. But they just shrugged and went back to discussing the merits of buffalo wings versus cocktail wienies.

Knowing Tom would be back in a few weeks gave Ryanne something to shoot for. She was sick and tired of looking like Ms. Potato Head, so she watched what she ate, and began walking up and down the country road early each morning. She forgave Tub Carver for setting up the wedding pool and shared diet tips with him. She considered regaining her prepregnancy figure a worthy goal. After all, Tom had never seen her figure and probably didn't know she had one.

She renewed her friendship with Kasey Tench who threw a blowout baby shower. Many of Ryanne's old friends showed up to offer their good wishes, and some even volunteered to baby-sit. Surrounded by people who cared for her, she no longer felt alone. She belonged to a vast, extended family. Thanks to their gifts of toys, clothes and baby gewgaws, Hannah had everything she needed.

Everything except a father.

Shortly after the shower, Gordon Pryor reported Josh had been located in Texas, performing in Matt Clancy's preshow band. He'd managed to dodge the process server, but Gordon promised that if they had to, they would slap him with the papers onstage.

She didn't tell the lawyer about the plagiarism. She wanted to confront her ex, get his side of the story. She didn't even mention it to Birdie. If the news got out, it would ruin his career. She didn't owe him anything, but he was Hannah's father, until he signed away his rights to the title.

She'd been angry when she first heard "Branded" on the radio. She'd worked so hard, sacrificed so much, for that opportunity. It made her sad to think that the man she'd once loved could be so ruthless. That he thought so little of her he would further his career at her expense.

But the anger was gone, displaced by amazing happiness that seemed to grow each day. The theft of her music was no longer significant. What were notes and words on paper, compared to what she had now? A beautiful baby, a community of caring people. A chance for a future with a man she loved.

She could only pity Josh, knowing how desperate he must have been to endanger his reputation so recklessly.

Checking with contacts in Nashville, she learned that singer Matt Clancy had indeed purchased the rights to "Branded" from Josh. Her ex had passed it off as his own for a tidy sum and a place on the tour. She'd known he was brash and irresponsible, but how could he be foolish enough to take credit for her music and risk a lawsuit? It was no surprise he had avoided the process server.

In mid-August, Tammy, the café's only waitress, went back to high school. Ryanne talked Birdie into letting her take her place for a while. She loved caring for Hannah, but she was getting cabin fever. A songwriter needed inspiration, and so far most of her compositions had been lullabies.

Hannah napped in a portable crib while Ryanne waited tables. Slipping into the rhythms of small-town life, she was surprisingly content. It was funny how unimportant the past became when the present was so full. She was no longer the insecure girl who feared failure and equated success with income and fame.

Every time she looked at Hannah's sweet face, she knew she'd found her fortune.

Anything else would be gravy.

One evening, after the last customer had left the Perch, Ryanne was alone at the counter, tallying the day's receipts. Hannah was beside her in the baby bouncer. When the bell over the door sounded, she spoke without looking up.

"Sorry. We're closed."

"Hello, Ryanne."

The sound of that voice startled her, and her head snapped up. "Josh. What are you doing here?"

He strode toward her, and she wondered how she'd ever found his loose-limbed swagger sexy. "We need to talk." He sat down in a back booth without waiting for an invitation.

"Coffee?" She felt surprisingly calm. The old Ryanne

would have lashed out at him, but now she knew better than to show her cards so soon.

"Got anything stronger?"

"I have a pot that's been sitting on the warmer a few hours," she said dryly.

"Whatever." He didn't smile as she placed two steaming mugs on the table.

Carrying Hannah, Ryanne sat opposite her ex-husband. "Like I said, what are you doing here?"

He looked at the baby, then at Ryanne. "I guess I wanted to make sure it's mine."

"It?" Ryanne bristled and started to rise. He put out his hand to stop her.

"Don't get all huffy. I know she's mine. I can see the resemblance."

"Do you want to hold her?" Hannah was a beautiful, perfect miracle, and she was his daughter. Surely he had some curiosity about her.

He shook his head. "I'd rather not."

Ryanne felt a surge of maternal protectiveness and knew she had to get rid of him. She had to get him out of Hannah's life, so her sweet little girl would never have to deal with his callous rejection. "So where are the papers?"

He removed the folded documents from his hip pocket and placed them on the table between them. "I couldn't believe you'd tell me like that. Damn, Ryanne. A process server."

Ryanne held Hannah close. "I guess we're even. I couldn't believe it when I heard Matt Clancy singing my song on the radio. What I did is completely legal. What you did, however, is not."

Josh's dark eyes narrowed. "I know it was wrong. But I used it to open doors. You know how it is. Things got out of hand. Now Clancy has offered me a slot in his own band. It's the best thing that's ever happened to me.''

She cradled her daughter who was the best thing to ever happen to *her*. ''I wonder what he'd think if he knew the truth.''

Josh's face blanched. ''That's another reason I'm here.'' He laid a second set of papers on the table. ''I got a lawyer, too. If you sign mine, I'll sign yours.''

''What are you talking about?'' Ryanne was losing patience with this man who had been her husband. They'd created a child together, but he was a stranger. She didn't like him very much.

He pushed a second document toward her. ''You agree to give up the rights to 'Branded' and never reveal the details of its sale. Also, you agree not to go public with the kid.''

''The kid?'' Ryanne tensed. ''She has a name, Josh. Her name is Hannah Rose.''

''Whatever.''

''Let me get this straight. You're willing to sacrifice your daughter to further your career?''

''You don't have to make it sound worse than it is.''

She didn't think she could do that. ''So, if I agree to what you're asking, you'll give up your parental rights? You'll stay out of Hannah's life? For good?''

''Yeah. That's about it.''

She yanked a pen out of her apron pocket, unfolded the papers, and scribbled her name on the bottom line. ''Done.''

''Don't you want to read it first?'' he asked.

''I trust you, Josh,'' she said with mock sweetness. ''You would never cheat me, would you?''

He winced at her words, but wasted no time signing

the papers Gordon Pryor had prepared. "I guess there's nothing left to say."

"Nope. Except I hope Clancy wins a Grammy with *your* song. It'll be quite a boost to your career."

"Don't hate me, Ryanne. I can help you. You're good, and I can get your stuff into the right hands."

She laughed bitterly. "You've certainly proven that. Thanks for the offer, but I'll find my own way." She picked up the papers that ensured Hannah a future without Josh's indifference. She wondered what she would tell her when she asked that inevitable question about why her father didn't love her.

She didn't know. But she had a few years to think of an answer that wouldn't hurt as much as the truth.

"I got the best of the bargain." She tucked the papers into her pocket. "You don't even know what you're giving up."

He looked at her with a sad expression. "Yeah, I do. I know exactly what I'm giving up."

Josh's unexpected appearance in the diner didn't become real to Ryanne until she delivered the signed papers to the attorney to file. When she stepped out of his office, her spirit shook off its burden and soared. The past was behind her now. She would take charge of the future.

Things were falling into place. Working with Birdie and Letha on the wedding plans, she discovered she had a natural talent for organizing such events. She and Birdie talked about starting a little catering business on the side. Not that there was a big demand for such services in Brushy Creek, but they could start small and grow.

And she didn't have to give up on her music, either.

She'd written several songs since Hannah's birth and sent them to a publisher in Nashville. She'd been astonished when he agreed to represent her. He gave her the name of a recording studio in Tulsa, and she was scheduled to cut a demo track of her songs. He thought her favorite piece, "What Do Babies Dream About?" could be marketed as a children's picture book, accompanied by an audiocassette of lullabies.

Junior and Letha invited her to sing at the wedding. With luck, it might lead to more requests to perform. Then there was teaching. Birdie had suggested she give violin lessons. She hadn't even advertised, and she already had two students lined up.

She could have the best of two worlds. Indulge her music addiction and be a good mother. Later, when Hannah was older, she could pursue a career if she still wanted it. She was proud of the fact that she'd worked it all out on her own. She was no puny damsel in distress now. She was close to being self-supporting. If she wasn't careful, people might even mistake her for a grown-up.

Life seemed full.

Except for the big, hollow place Tom had left when he breezed out of her hospital room with a promise to return.

She couldn't get those farewell kisses out of her mind, and the memory was making her crazy. She missed him more each day. Every time she had a small success, she longed to share it with him. She wanted him to be there, to delight in Hannah's progress.

But more than anything, she wanted Tom. She wanted to watch him work, knowing his long, hard body would soon lie next to hers. She wanted to make love to him while a warm summer breeze stirred the curtains. She wanted to hold his hand and watch their children grow.

She wanted what could be.

Chapter Twelve

Tom arrived in town early, the day of the wedding. He'd done what he set out to do. He'd tracked down two prize broncs, purchased them at bargain prices and delivered them, snorting, bucking, to a very happy stock contractor in Ft. Worth. The man was so pleased with his efforts that he offered Tom a full-time job.

Which he'd promptly declined.

He couldn't drive all over western creation, hunting down promising horses. He had plans in Brushy Creek. He had a house to build. A business to start. A life to live.

If what Pap reported was true, and Ryanne really was counting the days until he returned, he had accomplished his other objective. It had been hard to back off and give her the time and space she needed.

That day at the hospital, when Ryanne turned him down, he'd thought his heart would stop beating. How could she not love him, when he loved her so much? How could she not want him, when she was all he would ever want?

Then he'd had a Technicolor flashback of Mariclare angrily accusing him of thinking only of himself. Right before she'd walked out of his life forever. That's when he'd known. He'd been guilty as charged.

He'd come around, and realized how deep his feelings for Ryanne really were. He knew how much he wanted her and the baby in his life. He'd mistakenly assumed she knew it, too. That she wanted the same thing. He was ready to commit. He hadn't even stopped to consider that maybe she *wasn't*.

He'd been a fool to try to force her hand mere hours after she'd gone through the rigors of labor and delivery. The doctor had said it would take weeks for her whacked-out hormones to get back to normal. It had been grossly unfair of him to expect her to make a life-changing decision under such circumstances.

So, he'd left. He'd done the right thing for once in his life. He hoped like hell it wouldn't backfire on him.

As best man, Tom accompanied his father to the church where he donned a rented tuxedo. He stood before a mirror in the room assigned to the groomsmen, feeling big and awkward. He wasn't comfortable in formal wear, but if a pleated shirt and cummerbund was what it took to make Pap happy, then so be it. He pinned a white carnation in his father's lapel and gave him a congratulatory bear hug.

"You reckon we'll be having us another wedding in the family anytime soon?" Junior ran a finger under his shirt collar to loosen its death grip on his Adam's apple.

Tom grinned. "I hope so, Pap. But if we do, you can bet we won't be wearing these damn monkey suits."

His job was to hold the rings, keep the groom calm and get him to the altar on cue. But Tom was so nervous at the prospect of seeing Ryanne again, he wasn't much good for anything.

Then he heard her voice raised in song. He couldn't wait another minute; he had to see her. He left Pap and followed the sound to the sanctuary. There he stood in the back, and drank in the sight of her. She was everything his thirsty soul had hoped for.

He almost didn't recognize her, she'd changed so much in the month since he'd last seen her. A metamorphosis had taken place in his absence. Ryanne was no longer an adorable little egg. She'd cast off the shell and emerged as an impossibly beautiful, sexy woman.

His throat tightened as he took in the new Ryanne and made her a part of his memory. Her hair was a tumble of dark curls. Her dress, a simple, floor-length, sleeveless sheath, was the same emerald color as her eyes. The silky material draped her tiny figure, emphasizing curves he hadn't known she possessed.

She sat on a stool, accompanying herself on the guitar, and sang the Elvis Presley ballad "Love Me Tender" with heartfelt emotion. Her voice filled the small church which was packed with well-wishers. By the time she got to the second chorus, Tom saw the flash of hankies being whisked from breast pockets and patent-leather handbags, to dab at sentimental eyes.

That was the wonderful thing about Ryanne's musical gift. She possessed an unwavering ability to make her listeners feel the emotions of the words she sang. "Love Me Tender."

Forever, if she'd let him.

He knew the precise moment she became aware of him. A true professional, her expression didn't betray her. She did not miss a chord or fumble the lyrics. But as soon as her gaze found his, her eyes filled with light.

And he knew.

He *had* been right to stay away these past weeks. To give her a chance to find herself. To learn to stand on

her own. Physically she was transformed. But he knew
with a lover's certainty that the most important changes
were on the inside. She'd grown up. According to Pap,
she'd proved that by the mature way she handled the
confrontation with her ex-husband. She'd finally escaped
the shadows of the past.

All he wanted to do now was offer her the future.

Ryanne finished her song and sat in the front row
beside Birdie. Hannah was sleeping soundly in the older
woman's arms. Tom broke out of the trance he'd been
in and doubled back to walk his father to the altar.

The opening chords of the wedding march resonated
through the church.

Later, at the reception in the VFW hall, Ryanne
caught the bouquet through no fault of her own. The
new bride could not have tossed it more directly into her
hands without the aid of radar trajectory.

Ryanne's startled gaze met Tom's over the exuberant
collection of flowers, and her breath caught in her throat.
Who would have believed the rugged cowboy could look
so handsome in a tuxedo? He winked broadly, and she
felt the warm creep of color on her face.

What was he waiting for? Why didn't he try to talk
to her? She didn't have the courage to approach him. He
would have to come to her. She waited impatiently while
he toasted the bride and groom. Her foot was tapping
anxiously by the time Junior and Letha got around to
cutting Birdie's towering wedding cake.

She fielded compliments about her singing, agreed to
perform soon at the local beer joint and accepted two
new students, one for voice and one for violin.

Birdie had carried Hannah into a crowd of cooing
middle-aged matrons, leaving Ryanne all alone. She
stood off to one side of the room as the happy couple

took a slow turn around the dance floor. She felt oddly exposed and empty-handed, except for the rose and daisy bouquet.

Tom was busy being the best man, slapping shoulders, urging the guests through the buffet line. Speaking to the musicians. He'd shucked off his jacket, unbuttoned his collar and loosened his black tie, which hung loosely around his neck.

He was one sexy-looking cowboy.

What the hell was he waiting for?

The music started up again, and Tom approached Ryanne with a lopsided grin on his face. He made a gallant, if slightly overdone, bow and swept her onto the dance floor.

"Did you think about me while I was gone?" he asked without preamble, his words soft and warm on her neck.

"Maybe once or twice," she admitted. "In my spare time."

His hand pressed into her back and urged her even closer. She could feel the thrum of his heart under his fancy white shirt.

"Yeah. I hear you've been busy. Do you think you might be able to work me into your schedule?"

"It depends. What did you have in mind?"

He grinned. "It's only fair to warn you. Catching that bouquet marked the official beginning of our courtship."

Her heart sped up, then pounded with joy. Still, a girl had to play a little hard to get. "Is that a fact?"

"Yep. Just so there won't be any of those unfulfilled expectations you're so worried about, you need to know that I have dropped completely out of the buddy race. I am no longer willing to be your best friend."

He would always be her best friend. The one she could always depend on. She gazed up at him and saw the happiness in his eyes. She felt powerful, knowing she'd put it there.

"What are you willing to be?" She decided to play along. He'd obviously gone to a lot of trouble to set the stage.

He grinned. "A charming but relentless suitor who won't take no for an answer."

"I guess it would be pointless for me to fight it, then," she said with a resigned sigh.

"Don't give in too easily," he warned. "I plan to woo you."

"Woo me? Gosh. Do people still do that?"

"Oh, yeah."

His roguish glance raked her up and down, setting off the granddaddy of all twinges. Her pheromones went on instant red alert. Thank God everything was still in working order.

"Prepare to be wooed, lady. You're gonna get it all. Hearts and flowers. Balloons. Romantic dinners. Maybe even poetry."

"Poetry?" She fanned herself, a woman in danger of an imminent swoon. "You really are serious, aren't you, cowboy?"

He leaned down and whispered in her ear. "I have some courtship ideas that'll knock your socks off."

"Ooh." She feigned a shiver of excitement. "Is that the best you can do?"

He raised his brows at her teasing innuendo and pulled her tightly against his broad chest. "We're going to do it right this time."

She sighed. "Just so we do it."

He bent his head and captured her lips with his. She gave herself up to the moment, forgetting they were in the VFW hall, surrounded by wedding guests. The heat of his body woke her desire, and she knew in an instant that their life together would be a passionate one.

"I love you, Ryanne," he whispered. "You are the single most important fact of my life. I never want to be separated from you again. If you'll marry me, I'll do whatever it takes to make you and Hannah happy."

She smiled up at him. "I love you, too, cowboy."

He grinned. "We don't have to rush into anything. We can take it slow and easy."

She frowned. "Not *too* slow, I hope." She didn't want to wait any longer. The month-long separation had shown her how deeply she loved him. How much she wanted to build a life with him. With Hannah. With the children they would have.

She had no more doubts. She loved him. For all the right reasons. With her newfound maturity had come the realization that life—and love—followed its own secret timetable.

At Tom's cue the band segued into Patsy Cline's "Crazy." He held Ryanne's gaze as they danced over to Birdie. She gave them a big smile and thumbs-up, then placed little Hannah in the crook of his arm. He embraced Ryanne with the other, and without missing a step, waltzed the women he loved around the dance floor.

The other couples happily relinquished the floor and stepped aside with indulgent smiles. Out of the corner of her eye, Ryanne saw a small crowd congregate around Tub Carver.

It looked as if money exchanged hands.

* * * * *

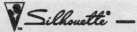

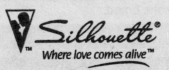